Anxiet

Anxiety Girl Series

Book 3

For Mum and Dad.

Thank you for making me believe that I *can* beat anxiety, each and every time it strikes.

FREEDOM IS NOTHING MORE THAN A STATE OF MIND.

Chapter 1

Staring into Aidan's dark eyes, I try to stop my heart from pounding as he looks back at me expectantly. Every emotion imaginable rushes through my veins, hampering my ability to answer his question. It's a simple enough question. Yes or no? An overwhelming combination of shock, joy and apprehension washes over me, momentarily taking away my ability to speak.

'Yes...' I manage eventually, breathing a sigh of relief at finally breaking the spell of silence. 'Of course, you can come in.'

Despite my efforts to step aside, I appear to be frozen to the spot as Aidan breaks into a huge grin.

'I was hoping you would say that.' Holding out Mateo, who has been quietly watching the scene unfold from his chest, Aidan grabs his backpack from the ground and hauls it over his shoulder.

A tiny *meow* snaps me back to attention and I somehow regain the use of my legs. Smiling back at Aidan, I motion for him to step inside the cottage. His familiar aftershave envelopes me in a comforting blanket as we come face-to-face in the hallway, neither one of us daring to breathe a word. His eyes burn into mine and I suddenly remember that I'm wearing my paint-splattered dungarees.

Self-consciously brushing my hair out of my face, my cheeks flush as I discover a blob of wet paint on the tip of my nose.

'I was going to mention that...' Aidan says teasingly.

Reaching out, he removes another smear of paint from my cheek and I feel my stomach flutter wildly.

'Aidan...'

Before I can say another word, a bang from the living room causes us to spring apart and I look down at the ground awkwardly as one of the builders strides out of the living room.

'The tiles for the kitchen have arrived.' Jason says cheerily, slipping a stubby pencil behind his ear. 'Do you want to take a look?'

Jason's thick Manchester accent brings me back down to Earth with a bump and I hastily clear my throat.

'I'll come through in a minute, thank you.' Forcing myself to smile, I nod as he disappears into the living room, leaving Aidan and I alone.

Waiting until the sound of Jason's footsteps fades into the distance, I turn back to Aidan.

'So...' He whispers, taking a step towards me as Mateo circles around us.

A flash of boyish laughter from the kitchen alerts me to the four burly builders on the other side of the wall and I quickly try to divert the conversation to a more platonic subject.

'I'm so pleased you have decided to settle in Cheshire, Aidan.' I say quietly, not wanting them to overhear our conversation. 'I'm sure you will be very happy here. Alderley Edge is a fabulous place to live.'

Aidan stares back at me intently, clearly wanting me to say more, but something inside me prevents me from doing so.

'Can I get you a cup of coffee?' I stammer, slipping my hands into the pockets of my dungarees awkwardly.

'Coffee?' Aidan repeats, his smile faltering for the first time.

Nodding back at him, I start to walk towards the kitchen without waiting for a response. As he follows my lead, I try to process what has just happened. Aidan is here. He's not in New Zealand. He's actually *here*, in Cheshire. He's in Alderley Edge. He's in Blossom View. He came back for... well, I don't know exactly what he came back for, but he's here.

Just fifteen minutes ago I was painting in the safety of my spare room. Now I am weaving through a minefield of paint pots and bricks to make coffee for the man I've spent the last few days obsessively thinking about. Reaching into my dungarees, I pinch myself and wince when my arm stings from my touch. How has this happened? *Why* has this happened? There are so many questions whirring around my mind and I don't have answers for any of them.

Stealing a glance at Aidan as Jason holds out a box of glistening ivory tiles, I peer at the carton as he waits for the verdict.

'Perfect.' I say confidently, quickly running my eyes over the box. 'They're exactly what I wanted.'

'Great stuff.' Placing the shiny tiles on the floor, he takes a chisel from his tool belt. 'So, you're happy for us to go ahead and take the others off?'

'Of course, but could you possibly salvage as many as you can?' I ask, continuing to tread through the building equipment. 'I'm thinking of upcycling them in the porch.'

'No problem. They should come off easily enough.' He replies with a grin. 'I'll tell the lads to be extra careful.'

'Thanks, Jason. You're a star.' Leaving him to get on with the renovations, I signal for Aidan to follow me into the back garden.

Allowing the kitchen door to close behind us, I lead the way along the cobbled path and take a seat on the bench by the blossom tree.

'You're going to need a lot more than that if you're going to settle down here.' I tease, pointing at Aidan's tired backpack as he sits down next to me. 'Where's your suitcase?'

'I took it back to The Shepard.' Aidan explains, laughing lightly as Mateo jumps up onto the bench.

'The Shepard?' I repeat, raising my eyebrows in surprise. 'You've been to The Shepard already?'

'I have. It was the first place I went from the airport.'

I smile in response, strangely disappointed at discovering I wasn't his top priority.

'I might have decided where I want to put down roots, but I still need a roof over my head while I set the wheels in motion.' Aidan explains, turning to face me. 'I thought you could help me with that, if you don't mind?'

Butterflies attack my stomach once more and I nod in agreement.

'It would be my pleasure...'

The two of us fall into an awkward silence as the sound of drilling drifts out of the cottage. I have pictured this moment in my mind so many times. What I would say to Aidan if I ever saw him again.

What I would have done differently if I could rewind the clock. Coulda, woulda, shoulda is all I have been able to think about, but now that he's right here next to me, I don't have a clue what to say. My mind is just blank, as though it's been wiped of all knowledge. Every single thing I wanted to say has been erased and in their place is an empty box, with nothing but random thoughts rattling around aimlessly.

'So, I see you made a start on the building work.' Aidan says, nodding politely at one of the builders as he drops a pile of bricks by the back door.

'I did.' I reply, relieved to have something to talk about. 'I hired the company you recommended.'

'Yes, I noticed their van outside.' Rubbing his hands together, Aidan squints at the label on the stack of bricks. 'How are you finding them?'

'They're very good. They've only been here for a couple of days, but they're making great progress already. I decided to go all out with the refurbishment, so they're going to be here a lot longer than I first anticipated.' I gush, very aware that I'm babbling. 'I didn't expect to have so many of them here. Every time I come home I seem to spot another new face, but they're all friendly enough. Jason brought doughnuts this morning and we discussed the plans for the kitchen over a coffee. Did you see Jason? He's the tall one with the dark...'

'Sadie?' Aidan interrupts gently. 'You're waffling. Are you okay?'

'I'm fine!' I lie, hoping he can't see past my strained smile. 'Honestly, I'm fine. I'm just... I'm just really surprised you're here.'

'I can't quite believe it myself.' Pulling Mateo onto his lap, he lowers his voice to a whisper. 'I questioned myself all the way back from the airport. *Am I doing the right thing? Is this really where my future lies? Would Mel approve of what I am doing*?'

My skin prickles at the mention of Mel and I bite my lip. Mel; Aidan's beloved late wife. What *would* she make of him restarting his life here?

'But as soon as you opened the door, all of my questions were answered.' He continues, his eyes softening as he stares at me. 'I just knew I had made the right decision. This is it. This is what it was all leading to. The only question I have now is, where do I go from here?'

'I thought you had decided to stay at The Shepard?' Flicking a piece of dried paint off my dungarees, I try not to show how happy this makes me. 'Your stuff is already there, you know it well and I'm sure Leonard will be glad of the business.'

'The Shepard is great, but I need to think of a more permanent solution.' Aidan replies breezily. 'I do love that location though. The countryside, the scenery, the raw openness of the place. It would be fantastic if I could find a property in that area.'

'Cheshire is a big place.' I explain. 'Don't limit yourself to one area. You haven't left the Golden Triangle yet.'

'And I don't think I need to. When you know, you know...'

Not daring to look directly at him, I hide behind my hair as my cheeks glow like hot lava.

'You know what I know?' I say suddenly, watching Mateo bound across the grass. 'I know that I need a drink.'

Aidan looks down at his watch and nods in agreement.

'It's five o'clock somewhere.'

Taking that as my cue to take charge of the situation, I clap my hands together and push myself to my feet.

'Since my kitchen is currently occupied, I vote that we go into the village. Just give me ten minutes to get changed and I shall be right back with you.'

'Have you been painting?' He asks, taking in my appearance for the first time.

'I *have* been painting. I woke up this morning and decided that today was going to be the day that I finally broke through the block and fell in love with art again.'

'And did you succeed?' His eyes crinkle into his smile as looks at me proudly.

'I think so.' My mind flits to the easel upstairs and I nod my head. 'I was actually lost in the canvas when you knocked on the door just now.'

'That's great!' He gushes, sounding genuinely happy. 'I'm so pleased for you.'

I grin back at him and start to walk towards the back door, before stopping and looking over my shoulder.

'Do you want to see?'

Not hesitating for a second, Aidan grabs his backpack and follows me into the cottage.

Slipping past the nattering builders, I head to the staircase and guide Aidan to the spare bedroom. The huge easel stands proudly in the centre of the empty room, displaying the work I fought so very hard to achieve. My heart throbs as I position myself next to the painting, secretly knowing Aidan was the inspiration behind it.

Carefully studying the canvas, Aidan's brow furrows into a frown and I suddenly worry that he can see himself in there. Between the splashes of black and smears of grey is my entire journey with him. From the day he walked into his first Anxiety Anonymous meeting to our last goodbye right here outside Blossom View. Every moment we shared, every conversation we had is displayed for the whole world to see, but the beauty is, only I know that. Only I know what I was thinking about as I brought the brush to the canvas. Only I know what this piece really symbolizes.

'It's... nice.' Aidan says uncertainly, squinting at a splodge of slate and nodding.

A smile plays on the corner of my lips as I watch Aidan try and fail to come up with more adjectives for my work.

'It's really... striking and... unique.' He manages, clearly struggling. 'It's...'

'Not quite what you were expecting?' I finish for him.

'Not exactly.' Aidan laughs and takes another glance at the easel.

I walk over to the cabinet and pull out a few more of my designs.

'I get that reaction a lot. You hear *artist* and immediately jump to Lowry and Leonardo da Vinci, but there is so much more to art than what you first think. Abstract breaks away from what people perceive to be the traditional representation of art and embraces a whole new world of beauty.'

Looking up, I'm surprised to see Aidan beaming down on me brightly.

'What?' I ask cautiously. 'Why are you looking at me like that?'

Before he can answer, an authoritative knocking interrupts our conversation.

'Yes?' I yell, my voice a few decibels higher than it usually is.

Placing my work on the dressing table, I smile as one of the builders pops his head into the room.

'The tiles are off now, so we're going to finish up and call it a night.' He says cheerfully, taking a screwdriver from his pocket and twirling it around his fingers.

'No problem. Will I be seeing you tomorrow?'

'Sure will. The kitchen units will be arriving in the morning, so I'll be here first thing with a handful of extra workers.' Nodding at Aidan, he smiles politely. 'Cheerio.'

'Bye!' I shout after him, waiting for the door to close before turning my attention back to Aidan. 'So, about that drink...'

Chapter 2

'What about this one?' I ask, leaning across the marble table and holding out my phone. 'It has three bedrooms, a garage and it's only a ten-minute drive from The Shepard.'

Abandoning his fork, Aidan takes the handset and flicks through the images on the screen. Quickly moving from one photograph to the next, he gives me the same expression he had in response to the other ten properties I've shown him.

'I think I need a car first to put *in* the garage.' He says with a slight smile, rubbing his temples wearily.

'You don't like it, do you?' Taking back the phone, I immediately bring up another listing. 'How about this one? Same area. It's in need of a little renovation work, but...'

I trail off as I realise Aidan doesn't appear to be as engrossed in this property search as I am.

'Am I giving you a headache?'

'No!' He protests weakly, reaching for his drink. 'It's just that it's been a pretty long day. This morning I was at the airport ready to fly to New Zealand and now I'm back here. It's a lot to process.'

Suddenly feeling rather silly for trying to railroad Aidan into purchasing a property so soon, I smile apologetically and drop the handset onto the table.

'Sorry, Aidan.' Pushing away my plate, I lean back in my seat and cringe with embarrassment. 'I'm getting a little ahead of myself.'

If you think the shock of discovering Aidan on my doorstep is what has made my behaviour become a little erratic, you would be correct. The truth is, if I don't fill the silences with talk of properties and business opportunities, my heart beats so fast I'm worried it might actually burst out of my chest. Obviously not having the same problem, Aidan sips his drink quietly, completely oblivious to my overwhelming levels of joy.

Trying to keep a calm exterior, I shuffle in my plush seat to get comfortable and look around the bar. It's been a long time since I last set foot in Precious and it's virtually unrecognisable from the place I remember. A wave of sadness hits me as I recall the last time I was here and I quickly shake it off. The new overhaul of the place has resulted in it looking a whole world away from what it used to. The walls are a pristine shade of white and the flooring is made up of gold mosaic tiles. The tables have been whitewashed, with centrepieces consisting of nothing more than a single white rose and the menus are carved into ragged slates.

'Sadie!' A welcoming voice yells in the distance, causing Aidan to look up from his drink. '*Sadie!*'

Knowing without turning around that this chirpy voice belongs to the owner, Patrick, I stand up as he rushes over to our table.

'Hi, Patrick!' Flashing him a friendly grin, I hold out my arms for a hug. 'How are you?'

'I'm good!' He trills, resting his hands on his hips theatrically. 'Look at you! You look incredible!'

Brushing off his compliments, I glance at Aidan as Patrick continues to shower me with praise.

'And who is this?' He exclaims, finally switching his focus to Aidan. 'I don't recall seeing you around here before...'

'Aidan's just moved into the area.' I explain, stepping back as Aidan stands up and shakes Patrick's hand firmly. 'Well, he's in the *process* of moving into the area.'

'Fantastic!' Patrick grins widely, giving Aidan a glimpse of his pearly whites. 'You'll love it here. Alderley Edge is just fabulous...'

'Actually, Aidan is interested in Mobberley. He's looking for a more rural location.' Retreating to my seat, I look on as Patrick reaches into the pocket of his shirt and produces a glossy card.

'Ah, you fancy throwing on some wellies and growing some crops?' He jokes, clapping Aidan on the back.

'Something like that.' Accepting the business card, Aidan studies the writing carefully.

'Give those a call and ask for Francesca.' Patrick instructs. 'Frankie has dealt with all our property affairs. Tell her I sent you and she'll look after you.'

'Thank you. I appreciate it.' Slipping the card into his battered leather wallet, Aidan smiles gratefully. 'I'll give her a call first thing tomorrow.'

'Thanks, Patrick.' I add.

'It's my pleasure!' Shaking his head, Patrick grabs a couple of cocktail menus from the table next to us. 'Now, you must allow me to get you some drinks. Have a look through the new menu and I'll bring them right over. I can especially recommend The Wizard.'

Very aware that Aidan has been yawning into his sleeve for the past thirty minutes, I know he won't want to work his way through Patrick's new cocktail menu right now.

'Maybe next time.' I reply, stifling a yawn of my own. 'It's been a rather long day.'

'Well, don't leave it too long. I miss seeing you down here.' Begrudgingly taking back the menus, Patrick sighs and tucks them under his arm. 'It was lovely to meet you, Aidan. Welcome to Cheshire!'

With a final double air-kiss, Patrick turns on his heel and sashays through the bar, greeting other customers as he goes.

'He seems nice.' Aidan remarks, dropping a handful of notes onto the table.

'He *is* nice. He's lovely.' Watching Patrick schmooze his clients with the utmost flair and prestige, I smile to myself and slip on my jacket. 'Are you ready to hit the road?'

'I am.' Aidan confesses, following me to the exit. 'Just point me in the direction of the nearest taxi rank and I shall bid you goodnight.'

'You don't need a taxi.' Plucking my car keys from the depths of my handbag, I twirl them around my fingers. 'I haven't been drinking virgin cocktails all evening for nothing.'

We step out onto the pavement and Aidan holds open the door for a young couple, who are chatting excitedly as they race down the steps into Precious.

'Are you sure?' He asks, looking left and right before crossing the road by my side.

'Positive.' Beeping open the car, I jump into the driver's seat and quickly fasten my seatbelt.

As Aidan buckles himself in, I pull away from the road and turn the radio up. Gentle music fills the car as I follow the winding road through the village. The sun set a short while ago, but the bright moonlight is highlighting the tops of the trees in an angelic haze, making it difficult to calculate whether it's early morning or late evening.

Indicating left, I look briefly at Aidan and notice his eyes close. Tiredness is etched into his face as his head dips lightly. The mental exhaustion is probably draining him more than the physical exhaustion right now. After a year of torment, the relief of finally settling on where his future lies must be a huge weight off his shoulders.

When I think back to the journey that led Aidan to my Anxiety Anonymous meeting, my heart aches with sadness. I'm incredibly proud of him for not allowing himself to crumble into a dark hole and wish away his future, but a part of me wonders how he is still standing. Just how does someone go through losing their wife in such a tragic way and not let it break them? Despite his world ending just twelve months ago, Aidan has fought his way through a forest of grief, anger and despair to battle his way to a future. A future he quite rightly deserves.

Lightly pressing the brakes, I rest my hands on the steering wheel as we come to a set of traffic lights.

'What are you thinking?' I ask, noticing Aidan is now awake and staring out of the window fixedly.

'I'm thinking that... I'm thinking that I can't quite believe I'm here.' He admits, running his fingers through his hair. 'Half of me doesn't want to go to sleep tonight in case I don't feel the same way in the morning...'

His words hit me like a bullet and I take a deep breath as the lights turn to green. Pressing my foot to the accelerator, I smile sadly and follow the curvature of the road.

'It's a big decision.' I mumble, turning down the radio. 'You're perfectly entitled to change your mind. You have to trust your gut and follow your heart.'

'It was my gut that led me back here.' Aidan says fondly.

'And your heart?'

'My heart never left...'

Managing a tiny smile, I keep my gaze fixed on the road ahead. *His* heart never left, but *my* heart left with him. Quite ironic when you think about it.

We turn onto the isolated country lane that leads to The Shepard and I put on the full beam headlights. Ruby's parents' farm stands authoritatively in the distance, surrounded by beautiful green meadows. Just knowing that Ruby is sprawled out on a Caribbean beach living her dream makes me feel all warm and fuzzy inside. Nothing has ever made me prouder than watching Ruby get ready to board that plane to Jamaica. All signs of the frightened young girl I first met had vanished and in their place was a strong and confident woman who was refusing to let the troubles of her past stand in her way.

Just like Aidan, Ruby is making a stand for what she wants and is prepared to put in the work to make it happen. I've always believed that if you are searching for that one person who will change your life, you should take a long hard look in the mirror. We all have the power to change the direction in which our lives are going, we just have to be strong enough to use it.

'How's your friend?' Aidan mumbles, as though reading my mind. 'Is she enjoying her trip?'

'She is.' I reply, happy that he remembered. 'The last time I spoke to her she was preparing to explore Dunn's River Falls.'

'Good for her. The falls are beautiful.' Aidan says between yawns. 'They're truly stunning...'

Gravel rumbles beneath the tyres as I bring the car to a stop in front of The Shepard and roughly pull on the handbrake. The dilapidated building is even more decrepit than I remember it.

'Remind me why you're staying here again?' I say with a frown, peering up at the tired structure dubiously.

'You really hate it, don't you?' Dragging his backpack onto his lap, he lets out a low laugh.

'No!' I protest, very aware that I don't sound convincing in the slightest. 'It's just that there are so many gorgeous hotels in the area...'

'Do any of these other hotels provide views like this?' He asks, pointing to the rolling landscape around us.

'Not quite...'

'Do they have they the privacy of this place?'

I look around the isolated bed and breakfast and shake my head.

'Do they...'

Holding up my hand to silence him, I turn off the engine and sigh.

'I get your point.'

Grinning back at me, Aidan reaches for the door handle and rests his fingers on the lever.

The silence quickly becomes deafening as I stare up at the sky and listen to the sound of the breeze as it wraps itself around the car.

'So...' I say casually, tapping my nails on the steering wheel. 'Where do we go from here?'

Taking a deep breath before speaking, Aidan scratches his stubble.

'Well, I'm going to go in here and you're going to head back to Blossom View.'

'And after that...'

Looking deep in thought, he unclips his seatbelt and shrugs his shoulders gently.

'To be completely honest, Sadie, I don't really know, but wherever I go, I hope you're going there with me.'

Blood rushes to my face for what feels like the millionth time today and I feel my stomach flip.

'I wish I could tell you I know what happens next, but the truth is, I don't. I'm not in any rush to purchase a place. If the right thing comes up tomorrow, I'll buy it tomorrow. If it takes twelve months, it takes twelve months. I've taken enough wrong turns in my life and I don't intend to take another.' Placing his hand on my forearm, Aidan smiles and shakes his head. 'You've been a great friend to me, Sadie, the best.'

My own smile wavers at the word *friend* and I feel my happiness fade slightly.

'I'll never be able to thank you enough for how much you have helped me.' He says seriously. 'No one will ever know what you have done for me. I don't think you're even aware yourself.' He continues, exhaling loudly. 'But *I* know and I will never forget.'

Attempting to dismiss his thanks, I cough awkwardly and make a stab at changing the subject.

'What are your plans for tomorrow?'

'Sleep, eat and scour the property listings.' Aidan replies, after taking a moment to consider my question. 'And you?'

'I am hosting the Anxiety Anonymous meeting in Wilmslow. You're welcome to come along, if you fancy joining us?'

'I think I am done with the support group for now.' Opening the door, Aidan tugs his backpack onto his shoulder. 'Sometimes the meetings bring up emotions I don't want to address, but I'll see how I feel.'

'Okay, but you shouldn't bury the emotions that scare you. The feelings you fight so hard to bury are usually the ones that are screaming out to be heard.'

'I get that, but I believe I've dealt with my issues and now I'm in a good place to move on. Yesterday is gone, no amount of counselling will ever bring it back. I'm ready to leave the past in the past and look forward to the future.'

'Well, if you do decide to join us, the meeting starts at one.' Resisting the urge to press him further, I turn over the engine. 'Just think, we could kill two birds with one stone and go over some property listings afterwards. The offer is there, if you change your mind...'

Stepping out onto the gravel, Aidan leans on the roof of the car and smiles.

'Thanks again, Sadie.'

'You're welcome. Anytime.'

Holding eye contact for a moment longer than necessary, I wave as he closes the door with a bang and takes a step back. From my rear-view mirror, I watch Aidan slowly walk inside the building. His tiny silhouette disappears into the distance as I fire along the empty lane, leaving nothing but a shadow where he once stood.

He's here. He's really here. Despite saying this over and over in my mind all day, I still don't believe it. The same tired backpack is on his shoulder, the same camouflage jacket on his back and the same... actually, he doesn't look the same at all. The constant pain in his eyes has vanished. The angst that clouded his face is nowhere to be seen. His voice sounds lighter, his shoulders appear looser and his entire demeanour is just... happier.

A rush of pride runs through me as I approach the lane that leads back to Blossom View. My work with Aidan is what has transformed him into the man he is today. I usually find it impossible to accept a compliment, but Aidan is right. *I have done that.* The reason he has turned his life around is that I helped him along the way and it feels so bloody good. Of course, it's my job to help people through their darkest days, but my relationship with Aidan goes deeper than a simple client/counsellor connection.

Aidan is my friend, he is someone I already feel an unbelievably strong bond with, and if his return to Cheshire is anything to go by, our relationship could take a turn we never expected...

Chapter 3

Peeling open my eyes, I fumble around on the bedside table for my mobile phone and lazily hit the snooze button on the alarm. The annoying chirping immediately silences as I roll over and yawn into my pillow. As usual, daylight floods into the bedroom through the stained-glass window, creating a pretty rainbow on the ceiling above me.

On a typical day, I would sleep for another half an hour or so, but with Jason and his team due to arrive at any moment, I don't want to be caught off-guard. Having your home invaded with balding, tea-swilling men, who crack crass jokes and enjoy toilet humour more than the rest of us is awkward enough, without having them discover you in your pyjamas.

Scanning the room for Mateo, I hang my head over the edge of the bed and lift up the sheets. Quickly discovering him curled up next to my suitcase, I reach out and stroke his silky fur. His white coat feels like velvet to my touch as I gently call his name to wake him from his slumber.

'Good morning!' I sing cheerfully, smiling when he stretches out his legs and effortlessly jumps up onto the bed.

His piercing blue eyes glint wildly as he paws the duvet before deciding the windowsill would suit him better for yet another snoozing session. Leaving him to enjoy his catnap, I throw back the duvet and push myself up. The plus side of being awake at such an ungodly hour is that I get the opportunity to enjoy something more than my usual boring apple for breakfast. The lure of a freshly-cooked breakfast courtesy of Aldo is one of the only things worth getting out of bed early for.

Due to his hectic work schedule, I haven't seen Aldo since my now infamous date with Pierce Harrington, so that should provide us with some rather interesting conversation points. My rejection of the perfect Pierce did not sit well with Aldo and I am yet to face the music for shunning who Aldo perceived to be my perfect match. As much as I am dreading the ear-bashing I'm no doubt going to receive about Pierce, I'm even more nervous to tell him about Aidan's return to Cheshire.

Aldo has made no secret of disliking Aidan from the very beginning and I guess I can understand why. Aidan is moody and mysterious in a way that other men find intimidating, but he does have a heartbreaking reason why. His refusal to let his guard down results in him being perceived as aloof, standoffish and dare I say it, a little strange. Aidan might have chosen to let down his walls and allow me to see the real him, but he is yet to give the rest of the world the same privilege.

Realising I could be inundated by a swarm of workmen at any given second, I force myself to put one foot in front of the other and wander into the bathroom. The same loose floorboard squeaks under my weight as it does every morning and I make a mental note to ask one of the builders to take a look at it. Blossom View might be a work in progress, but despite the old features and worn fittings, it already feels like home to me. Unlike anywhere I've ever been before, the cottage has a way of wrapping its arms around you and making you feel shielded from the rest of the world. When I am here, nothing else seems to matter. I'm not counsellor, friend, or partly-estranged daughter. I am simply Sadie Valentine. I can be completely myself and that is a joy most people don't get to experience...

After a quick shower, I run a toothbrush over my teeth and head back into the bedroom in search of a suitable outfit. No sooner have I wiggled my way into a pair of skinny jeans and tugged on a simple black jumper there's a knock at the door. The sound of van doors slamming shut leaves me in no doubt as to who has arrived.

Rushing down the stairs as quickly as my legs will carry me, I throw open the door to reveal a very happy Jason.

'Morning, Sadie!' He says, expertly holding an enormous set of ladders over his shoulder. 'We've brought in the cavalry today...'

Looking past him, I'm surprised to see at least five other builders pouring out of the vans that have pulled up at the side of the road.

'Hello...' I say timidly, stepping back as they pile into the cottage.

'The guys have had another job cancel.' Jason explains, nodding to one of the builders as he holds up a scary-looking piece of equipment. 'So we're going to double up on yours today.'

'I see.' Smiling at the men as they immediately down tools and get to work in the kitchen, I catch a fleeting glance of one of the builders and try to work out why he looks so familiar.

'Don't worry, love.' Jason laughs, popping my thought bubble. 'I'll make sure they're on their best behaviour.'

Laughing along with him, I close the door and tuck my wet hair behind my ears.

'Can I get you all a drink?'

'No need. We've come prepared.' He points to a flask next to his feet and grins before joining the others in the kitchen.

Deciding to leave them to it, I run back upstairs and grab my hairdryer. Despite having my hair cut short just six months ago, it's growing back with a vengeance. It's hard to believe my long locks were once a shoulder-length bob and it's even harder to believe why. Since crawling out of the dark world of anxiety, my life has gone from strength to strength and apart from the odd wobble here and there, I'm proud to say I've been anxiety-free.

Blasting my hair with the hairdryer, I grab a paddle brush and wonder what Aldo would say if he could see how badly I am treating my hair. Being a hairdresser to the stars means he expects everyone to have perfectly coiffed locks at all times, but if life has taught me anything, it's that *good enough* is *good enough*...

* * *

'What the hell have you done to your hair?' Aldo grumbles, jabbing a piece of halloumi with his fork.

Reaching for my coffee cup, I roll my eyes and brush a frizzy strand of hair out of my face.

'I wondered how long it would take for you to notice.'

'Believe me, I can spot the absence of heat protection spray a mile away...'

I place my fork on my plate and narrow my eyes at my best friend. His pretty face crumples into a frown as he catches sight of his reflection in the mirror and adjusts his ponytail. A glimpse of a tattoo creeps over the edge of his collar, providing a hint of the inked body that is underneath.

'Let's not pretend this is about my split ends.' I sigh, pulling the sleeves of my jumper over my hands. 'We both know this has far more to do with Pierce Harrington than it does my lack of hair maintenance.'

Aldo crosses his legs petulantly and digs his phone from his pocket.

'Pierce is perfect.'

'He *is* perfect.' I agree, wiping the corners of my mouth with a napkin. 'He's just not perfect for me.'

'How can he not be for you?' He exclaims in frustration. 'He's handsome, rich, funny...'

'Then why don't you date him?' I fire back, thanking the waitress as she removes our empty plates.

'I don't think he swings my way.' Aldo grumbles. 'More's the pity...'

'When has that ever stopped you from trying?' Looking at my watch, I attempt to move the conversation along. 'How's Edward?'

'Don't try changing the subject. I'm not done with you yet.' Leaning forward in his seat, Aldo scratches his tattoo-covered knuckles. 'If Pierce isn't what you're holding out for, who is? Who is ever going to be good enough for you?'

I raise my eyebrows and look around the busy café, searching for an answer to the question I've asked myself a hundred times already.

'Tom Hardy? David Gandy? Ryan Gosling? Ramos with the Bugatti Veyron? The hot banker who comes into the salon? That weird loner guy you ran off to Surrey with...'

'I didn't *run off* to Surrey with Aidan!' I protest. 'I was helping him to grieve the loss of his wife!'

'Whatever.' Aldo replies haughtily. 'Answer my question. Who are you waiting for?'

Tearing my eyes away from his, I watch the steady stream of people rush past the window and wonder if I should tell him about Aidan moving to Cheshire. It's the perfect opportunity. Aldo brought him up and it would certainly take the attention away from my grilling over Pierce.

I think back to the moment I discovered Aidan on my doorstep yesterday and something inside me becomes rather protective.

'When I find him, I'll let you know!' I say lightheartedly, reaching under the table for my handbag. 'Are we having a look around the shops or are you going to stay here sulking over a man who was never yours to lose?'

Responding with nothing more than one of his trademark sneers, Aldo grabs his leather jacket from the back of the seat and follows me out onto the street.

'Where are we heading first?' I ask, linking my arm through his.

'The salon. If I have to look at that frazzled mop of yours for a second longer, I'm going to rip it out.'

Letting out a shocked scoff, I bat his arm playfully and allow him to drag me across the busy road. As much as I believe my hair is perfectly acceptable, I'm secretly delighted to be treated to one of Aldo's signature blow-drys. Plus, if anything is going to turn that frown of his upside down, it's being in the place he loves the most, doing what he does best.

'Where is everyone?' I ask, stepping into the glistening salon and realising it's completely empty.

'We changed the opening hours last week. We don't open for another hour.' Pushing back the flowing drapes, he signals for me to get into a chair. 'These hours suit our clients more. Later starts, longer nights.'

Nodding along, I can't help thinking the change in opening hours has more to do with Aldo's love of tequila and dancing on tables and less to do with his clients' work schedules.

'What are we doing?' He asks, as I twirl around in the leather chair. 'Do you fancy going back to the lob?'

Stopping in front of the mirror, I stare at my reflection as a flashback to the last time Aldo cut my hair comes flooding back to me. The angst, the sadness and the crippling anxiety just fell away with each snip of the scissors. My new hair was a significant part of my journey back to mental wellness. It marked the start of a new phase in my life. Freeing myself of my long hair was my way of letting go of what was such a horrendous time for me and moving on.

'No.' I say with confidence. 'I've decided to grow it out.'

'Really?' Aldo replies sceptically, picking up a few strands of my hair and scrutinising the ends. 'The lob looked so much better.'

Frowning back at him, I grab a magazine from the stack to my left and flip through the pages.

'Just a trim, thank you very much. Let's not go crazy...'

'You're not planning on letting it get back to what it used to be, are you?' He grumbles, gathering a selection of scissors and brushes on the table next to us.

'That's exactly what I'm planning on doing.' Sticking my tongue out at him, I stand up as he holds out a black cape. 'You do know I've just washed my hair, don't you?'

'Washed?' He repeats, a look of horror on his face. 'Don't make me laugh! A quick rinse with the shower head does not count as *washed*. Get to the basin.'

Not being able to argue with him, I do as I am told and follow him across the salon floor.

'So, where the hell were you yesterday?' He asks, turning on the water and adjusting the temperature. 'I called by your place, but you weren't home.'

A pang of guilt hits me as I look up at the huge chandelier and think back to my meal with Aidan.

'Spit it out, Shirley.' Massaging raspberry shampoo into my scalp, Aldo leans over and gives me a knowing glare. 'Stop searching for a lie and just hit me with it.'

Cracking my knuckles anxiously, I curl my lip into a tiny smile.

'I went for dinner with Aidan...'

'With who?' He demands, reaching for the conditioner.

'Aidan.' I repeat. 'The guy from Anxiety Anonymous. The one I went to Surrey with.'

Aldo's hands freeze on my head and I immediately regret being honest with him.

'I thought he had gone to New Zealand?'

'So did I, but he changed his mind.'

'Please tell me you're not dating him.' Aldo groans, attacking my hair with the water tap once more.

'Of course, I am not dating him!' A laugh escapes my lips as Aldo peers down on me suspiciously. 'We're just... friends.'

My conversation with Aidan outside The Shepard comes back to haunt me and I feel my smile drop. *You've been a great friend to me, Sadie, the best.*

'Well, you better stay just friends.' Aldo warns sternly. 'The guy gives me the creeps...'

Finally turning off the water, he wraps my hair in a towel and beckons me to follow him back to the chair.

'Aidan's a great guy, Aldo.' I say casually, wiping a bead of water from my temple. 'You just need to give him a chance and you will see that for yourself.'

Dragging a comb through my wet hair, Aldo spins my chair around narrows his eyes.

'Why do I get the feeling you're keeping something from me?'

Opening and closing my mouth repeatedly, I cover my eyes with my hands.

'How? How do you do that?'

'Do what?'

'Know when I'm hiding something...'

'If I told you, I'd have to kill you. Come on, spit it out.'

Reaching for the colour wheel, I run my fingers over the many different swatches and lower my voice to a whisper.

'He's moving to Cheshire.'

'And?' Aldo presses.

'And I am helping him to find a place.'

'And?'

'And *nothing*, that's it.' I say honestly, turning back to face the mirror.

'If that's the case, why were you hiding it from me?' He demands, expertly flipping my hair back and forth before settling on a centre parting.

'Because you don't like him.' Pretending to be engrossed in the hair samples, I hold the chart an inch from my face and study the options. 'I didn't want you to give me a hard time about it.'

'Just don't be getting too emotionally involved with anyone right now.' Aldo says, dividing my hair into tiny sections. 'You've done so well...'

Here we go again. The *you've done so well* speech.

'You've really turned your life around. I don't want you to lose your job for breaking some kind of rules...'

'First of all, you had no problem with me becoming *emotionally involved* with Pierce.' I reply smugly, counting my points off on my fingers. 'Aidan and I are just friends. There is no rule that says you cannot be friends with attendees. Second of all, Aidan is no longer an attendee.'

Taking his scissors, Aldo gently pushes my head down and mumbles something I don't quite catch in response.

'Either way, Shirley, I don't like the guy.'

Choosing not to reply, I peer through my hair as Aldo gets to work at transforming my bedraggled hair into a masterpiece. Apart from tequila, tattoos and male models, there isn't much Aldo does like. If it doesn't get him drunk, permanently scar his body or give him a night to remember in an outrageously expensive hotel suite, he just isn't interested.

Most friendships are built on a mutual respect for one another, honesty and trust. Ours? Well, ours is built on a solid foundation of alcohol, excruciatingly-tight jeans and a shared love of the black manicure, but I wouldn't have it any other way...

Chapter 4

Organising the ever-growing pile of paperwork in the meeting room, I lean across the information stand and pull on the cord to open the blinds. The Anxiety Anonymous meeting starts in just five minutes and the seats are already starting to fill up. A few recognisable faces are in their usual places, quiet chatter drifts through the air and a couple of nervous new attendees are hovering in the doorway.

'Is this your first time with us?' I ask a petite blonde lady, who is holding on to the information stand looking absolutely petrified.

A slight nod of the head confirms to me that it is.

'Okay. Please take a seat wherever you feel the most comfortable. Or, if you prefer, I could move a chair to the back of the room and you can simply watch how this initial meeting pans out.' I offer, flashing her a welcoming smile.

'That would be great.' Cautiously looking around the busy room with wide eyes, she nods once more. 'Thank you.'

Taking a chair from the far side of the circle, I position it next to the coffee station and signal for her to sit down.

'There's no pressure whatsoever. Just sit back and get a feel for the place. If you want to contribute, feel free to do so. If you decide this is not for you and want to slip out halfway through, that's fine also.'

Smiling gratefully, the blonde lady gingerly takes a seat and rests her handbag on her lap. When I first took over from Julia, nervous attendees were my worst nightmare. Being an ex-member myself, I know how daunting it is to walk into this building for the very first time, and I also know absolutely nothing I say will ease her angst. The trepidation of coming to a support group such as Anxiety Anonymous is almost as bad as the anxiety itself. The feelings you're trying to escape make themselves known, louder and more frightening than they were before. The racing heart, the churning in your tummy, the sweaty palms and the all-encompassing sense of nausea that takes over your ability to function like a human being should.

I want to tell her that things will get better. I want to tell her that over time, her symptoms will slowly fade away and she will be able to return to the best version of her. The version of herself that she is craving to be. I want to tell her that making the decision to walk through the door here today will pave the way to a brighter future, but I know it won't help. To conquer anxiety, we must first *believe* that we can conquer anxiety, without simply believing what others tell us.

Leaving her to settle in, I take my place at the front of the room and look up as the door squeaks open once more.

'Yvette!' I say in surprise, completely floored to see her here. 'Hi! How are you?'

'I'm fine...' Juggling a stack of folders, Ruby's mother tugs her handbag onto her shoulder and smiles awkwardly.

After Yvette's first visit to the support group a couple of weeks ago, I didn't expect to see her again, but she's continuing to prove me wrong. She attended the last meeting of her own free will and here she is again.

'I'm so glad you came!' I exclaim, rushing over and taking the files from her. 'What have you got here?'

'I was reading up on herbal medications for anxiety.' Yvette explains, flipping open one of the folders. 'Then I stumbled across all these different breathing techniques and mindful activities. I thought you could put them on the information stand.'

'This is fantastic!' Genuinely touched that she's taken such a keen interest, I place the folders on my desk. 'What a great idea.'

'Do you really think so?' Beaming proudly, Yvette hands over yet more printouts.

'I do! Ruby would be so proud of you.'

'I hope so. After all, she's the reason I'm here...' With a final grin, Yvette excuses herself and walks away to join the rest of the group.

Watching her mingle with a few people she recognises from previous meetings, I smile to myself happily. The difference in Yvette really is remarkable. Just a short while ago, Ruby's mother was completely blind to the plight of her daughter and other anxiety sufferers, yet coming to the meetings has enabled her to discover exactly what anxiety is and just how deeply it can affect a person.

I wish I could say the same for my own mother, but one single meeting was all it took for her to declare she knew everything there was to know about anxiety. To be fair to her, she *has* made the effort to be more present in my life lately, but as far as her attempts to understand mental health go, I'm afraid she's fallen at the first hurdle. A hurdle most people seem to find so very tricky to master.

Bringing my wandering mind back to the meeting, I look at the clock and let out a disappointed sigh. With just a few minutes to go, it seems that Aidan isn't going to show and of course, that's perfectly okay. Peering out of the window, I picture him at The Shepard, sitting on the terrace and looking out over the open fields that he loves so much.

Of all the people I've met here at the support group, Aidan is my best success story date. To have witnessed his transformation from heartbroken widower in the grips of despair, to the man who can smile and actually mean it has been truly remarkable. Turning back to face the room, I place my hand over my heart and make it my mission to replicate this feeling for every single person in front of me. Right on cue, the circle falls into silence, signalling it's time for the meeting to begin.

'Alright, let's get this show on the road...'

* * *

The meeting ended a few minutes ago and as usual, a cluster of attendees have stayed behind to enjoy the complimentary snacks and beverages. Slipping on my jacket, I watch as Yvette offers her makeshift information packs to the remaining members in the room and flash her the thumbs-up sign. Unlike when the meeting is in action, the atmosphere is light and airy, creating a friendly ambiance for people to forget about why they're here and just enjoy a moment to themselves.

Not wanting to interrupt, I leave them to chat and make my way along the dimly-lit corridor. Pausing by the exit, I adjust my collar before pulling open the door and stepping outside.

'Aidan!' I exclaim, unable to hide how happy I am to see him. 'Hi! How long have you been here?'

Shrugging his shoulders, he smiles and looks at his watch.

'Not too long.'

'You didn't fancy joining us?' I ask, folding my arms and grinning inanely.

'Not today, but never say never.' Aidan replies easily. 'Are you still free for lunch?'

Nodding back at him, I give him a quick once-over and realise how very different he looks. Wearing a pair of slim-fitting jeans with a crisp white shirt, he looks worlds away from his normal distressed style. His curly hair is brushed back off his face and his usual stubble is non-existent. He looks years younger than he did yesterday. Years younger and ten times as relaxed.

'You've changed your hair.' He remarks, giving me a cursory glance as we head across the car park.

Suddenly remembering my voluminous curly blow-dry courtesy of Aldo this morning, I self-consciously smooth it down.

'Thank you.' I reply, blushing at his compliment. 'We could try The Secret Garden for lunch. The food is fabulous and it should be quiet, so we could go through the property listings as well.'

'Sounds good to me.' Pausing to let a car pass before we cross the street, Aidan falls into step next to me. 'You're the expert around here.'

'And once I am done with you, *you* shall be, too.'

Pulling open the door to The Secret Garden, I squeeze past the flowerbeds and take a seat in a secluded booth next to the window. Delicate fairy lights hang from the ceiling, giving the illusion we're dining alfresco and not in a high-end restaurant in the centre of Wilmslow.

Quickly ordering a bottle of water for the table, I check my phone for emails as I wait for Aidan to study the menu.

'Alright...' I say excitedly, pulling my laptop out of my bag. 'The listings are updated on a daily basis, so there should be a whole new bunch of properties to look at. Did you keep the card from Patrick?'

'I did.' Reaching into his wallet, Aidan takes the glossy card and slides it across the table. 'I had a look on their website this morning. They have a barn conversion that I wouldn't mind taking a look at.'

'Great!' I reply, tapping at the keyboard and bringing up the website to see for myself. 'Which barn conversion? This one?'

Turning the screen around to face him, I scroll through the pictures as he nods along.

'It needs a *lot* of renovation work doing.' I remark, pausing on a picture of a bathroom that resembles something from a horror movie. 'Are you willing to take on such a huge project?'

'I think so.' Studying the photos in great detail Aidan nods in approval and clicks on the next image. 'I was thinking about going into property development. Just small ventures to begin with. I could buy a real fixer-upper, fill my time with the renovations and sell it on for a profit.'

'When did you decide this?'

'Last night.' Aidan admits, thanking the waitress as she places two glasses of water on the table. 'My finances allow me to do it and it would be a great way to get to know the area better.'

'I think it's a brilliant idea.' Writing the listing number on a sticky note, I smile encouragingly. 'Plus, it's just minutes from The Shepard. It's *exactly* where you wanted to be. Should I give them a ring and arrange a viewing?'

Resting his elbows on the table, Aidan closes his menu.

'You don't have to do this, you know? You've already done so much for me.'

'Don't be silly. It's my pleasure.' Taking the contact card, I punch the number into my phone and hold the handset to my ear. 'After all, what are friends for?'

Aidan opens his mouth to say something, but before the words can escape his lips a gentle voice floats down the line.

'Hello?'

'Hi! Is that Frankie? It is? Fantastic. My name is Sadie Valentine. I am calling on behalf of a friend. Patrick Kelly gave me your details...'

As I arrange a viewing with the ever-so-helpful Frankie, Aidan places an order with the waitress and looks through the barn images once more.

Thanking Frankie for her assistance, I end the call and scour the table for my menu, which seems to have disappeared.

'I ordered for both of us.' Aidan says apologetically. 'I hope you don't mind?'

'Oh...' A little taken aback, I smile and shake my head. 'Not at all. What did you go for?'

'The bruschetta, followed by the sea bass. We can go change it, if you would prefer?' He stammers, seemingly a little embarrassed. 'I'm sorry. It's just that I used to order for Mel whenever we ate out. This is the first time I have dined out with someone since she...'

'Aidan, you don't have to explain yourself.' I say gently. 'Besides, the bruschetta is my favourite thing on the menu and the sea bass is a speciality of theirs. I couldn't have chosen anything better myself.'

Staring into the bottom of his glass, Aidan sighs as a slight frown creeps onto his face.

'What did the estate agent say?'

'I've arranged a viewing for tomorrow at two.' I reply, scribbling the time of the appointment down on a napkin. 'Frankie said she will meet us there. Sorry, she will meet *you* there...'

'You're not coming along? Do you already have plans for tomorrow?'

'Erm...' My stomach churns and I pull my own glass towards me. 'It's actually my day off tomorrow, but you don't want me there cramping your style...'

'Nonsense! I could do with a second opinion.'

Closing my laptop, I decide not to protest any further.

'Do you have a car now?'

'I hired one this morning.' Aidan explains, folding the napkin into a tiny square. 'I've got such a good feeling about this barn conversion. It ticks so many boxes...'

As Aidan continues to tell me about his hopes and dreams for the viewing tomorrow, I nod along and look around the room. Despite being fairly empty, one rather loud table are making enough noise to fill the entire restaurant. Their high-pitched cackles cut through the air as they clink their glasses together and whoop raucously.

Trying to concentrate on what Aidan is saying, I twirl my straw around my glass and feel my jaw drop open. As the waiter walks away from the table in question, I am given a glimpse of the noisy party. With matching tousled hair extensions and undeniable mean girl cackles, Piper, Ivy and Zara are unmistakeable. It's been months since I last laid eyes on the terrible three, but it feels like only yesterday. The same heavily-contoured makeup is plastered on their faces, the same sickly-sweet perfume is surrounding them and the same Chanel handbags are resting by their feet. Whereas my life couldn't look more different from how it did a year ago, it seems not much has changed for my ex-friends. In fact, it appears nothing has changed at all.

Very aware that I'm staring, I try to drag my eyes away, but I seem to be frozen in shock. Details of the last time I saw them come rushing back to me as a cold sensation hits my gut. Their disinterested sneers, their condescending laughs, their ability to make me feel an inch tall when I was already feeling lower than I've ever felt before. The searing pain that ripped through my heart when I realised Ivy had been dating Spencer behind my back. The devastation that hit me when Piper laughed at my revelation of suffering from anxiety. The tears I cried when it finally hit me that these girls were never my friends at all...

Suddenly turning around, Piper reaches into her handbag and looks directly at me. Our eyes lock, both of us looking equally startled as we stare at each other in complete silence. One by one, Ivy and Zara mimic Piper's actions and join in with the staring competition.

Slowly raising her hand, Piper offers me a tiny wave and the other two follow suit. Not knowing how to respond, I look back at them blankly until the sound of Aidan's voice breaks the connection.

'Sadie? Sadie, are you okay?'

Quickly snapping back to attention, I force myself to smile and nod.

'Are you sure?' He presses, clearly concerned. 'You look like you've seen a ghost.'

The truth is, I *have* seen a ghost. I've seen three. But unlike the ghosts that I fear on the silver screen, I refuse to be haunted by them any longer. I can't change the past, I can only change the way I decide to move on from it. There's no point in opening old wounds just to be cut even deeper in the future. Life sends us lessons to learn from, to grieve over and to teach us to never make the same mistake again...

'I'm fine. It's just some people that I used to know.' Shaking off all thoughts of days gone by, I focus on

Aidan and take a deep breath. 'Now, about this barn conversion...'

Chapter 5

Gathering the pile of letters from their resting place on the doormat, I flip through the envelopes and immediately discard anything I recognise as junk mail. The rhythmical banging from the kitchen is gradually becoming a normal part of my morning routine and as a result, I'm able to get through my boring admin work with minimal disruption.

Tucking the letters under my arm, I sit down on the couch and reach for my coffee cup. Despite a rather miserable weather forecast, it has turned out to be a beautiful day. Sunshine is blaring into the living room and the blue sky is harbouring just a single lazy cloud. Looking out of the window, I smile at the sight of two robins flitting around the front garden and position a cushion behind my back.

'*Meow...*' Mateo purrs, nuzzling his pink nose against my hand.

Scratching his fluffy belly, I wiggle my fingers over his head as he rolls onto his back and bats my hand gently. Never one to shy away from a fight, Mateo furiously attacks my fingers until he decides he's had enough and flips back over onto his belly. With a final *meow*, he curls up on the cushion next to me and closes his eyes.

Taking the hint, I return to my mail and tear open the first envelope. Discovering my usual bank statement, I toss it onto the coffee table and reach for the next. Before long, I have a mountain of invoices, card statements and insurance documents piled up in front of me. Telling myself I will deal with them later, I reach for the final letter and turn it over in my hands.

Unlike the others, this one is handwritten and much thicker, signalling something more exciting could be waiting inside. Slipping a finger under the tab, I pull out the contents and frown as a bunch of leaflets fall into my lap along with a crisp letter.

Carefully unfolding it, I squint at the text and take a sip of coffee.

'Sadie...

...Please find enclosed flyers for the annual Anxiety Anonymous fundraiser...

...Our charity fundraisers are always a huge success and this year, I am leaving the Alderley Edge fundraiser in your very capable hands...

...I apologise for the short notice period, but you will be glad to hear that all plans are already in place...

...All I require from you is to spread the word...

...The venue has been arranged and the acts have been booked...

...If local businesses would like to take part by donating prizes for the raffle, that would be great...

...If there's anything you would like to add, or any members of your support group would like to get involved in any way, that would be great also...

...Please feel free to put your own stamp on the event...

...The information you shall need regarding the event schedule is at the bottom of this letter...
...All monies raised will help us to open new branches of Anxiety Anonymous across the United Kingdom...
...Spread the word, have fun and enjoy the fundraiser...'

Folding the letter neatly, I place it back into the envelope and pick up the leaflets. It seems Julia really *has* taken care of everything. According to the pamphlets, the fundraiser is going to take place next week and will involve everything from raffles and cake stalls, to face painting and balloon twisting. All there's left for me to do is sell the tickets and hopefully wangle a few donated items in the process.

Adding the fundraiser to my to-do list, I take a couple of the leaflets and head into the kitchen.

'How are you getting on in here?' I ask Jason, who is busily cutting down tiles by the back door. 'It looks like you're making good progress.'

'It's coming along well.' Pausing to wipe his brow on his sleeve, Jason nods and leans against the doorframe. 'The corner unit was causing us a little trouble, but Gav's shaving it down to fit.'

He points to another builder in the garden and I realise it's the same guy I thought I recognised a couple of days ago. I can't see his face, but the niggling thought of where I know him from is beginning to annoy me. Straining my neck to get a better look at him, I frown when he downs tools and disappears to the van.

'That's fantastic...' I reply, placing the fundraiser leaflets on the fridge with the help of a magnet. 'Where is your company based again?'

'Prestwich.' Jason says, reaching for his flask. 'Why, do you know it?'

Nodding my head, I lean against the sink and bite my lip.

'Sort of. My mum and I used to live in Middleton many years ago.'

'Ah...' He says knowingly. 'Big change.'

'Very.' Not wanting to get into the ins and outs of how we ended up in the Golden Triangle, I decide to steer the conversation back to the renovations. 'So, what's next on the agenda, you know, after the kitchen is completed?'

Taking a pencil from behind his ear, Jason taps it against the windowsill.

'Erm, we'll probably make a start on plastering the dining room. All being well with the damp proofing, of course...'

'Of course.' I repeat authoritatively, as though I know exactly what I am talking about. 'Anyway, I should probably leave you to it. I have to nip out for a couple of hours, but if I'm not back by the time you guys have finished, I shall see you tomorrow.'

'No problem.' Putting his flask down, Jason returns to cutting the tiles. 'See you tomorrow, love.'

With a final glance at a snoozing Mateo, I grab my handbag and make my way along the garden path to my car. The impressive trees that line the winding lane are almost in full bloom, creating a beautiful avenue of leaves. Their branches intertwine seamlessly, shielding me from the traffic on the road as I jump into the driver's seat and fasten my seatbelt.

I am due to meet Aidan at the barn conversion in fifteen minutes, which gives me just enough time to make the drive over there. Releasing the handbrake, I turn onto the open road and press my foot to the floor. The sun peeks through the trees, lighting up the road as I race by and happily sing along to the radio.

Pausing at a set of traffic lights, I tap my fingers on the steering wheel in time to the music and wait for the stream of people to cross the street. Too busy admiring a passing poodle's flawless perm, I almost don't notice my phone is ringing on the seat next to me.

Hitting the hands-free icon on the steering wheel, I turn down the radio before speaking.

'Hello?'

'Sadie? Where are you?'

'Hi, Mum. I'm just driving at the moment...'

'What's all that noise?'

'What noise? The barking? Oh, there's a dog walker crossing the street. Is everything okay?'

Lifting my foot off the brake as the lights change to green, I take a left and head towards Mobberley.

'Oh... Anyway, I was wondering if you would like to go for lunch?'

I feel my lips spring into a smile at her offer and I nod in response, momentarily forgetting that she can't see me.

'Of course, when were you thinking?'

The fact that my mother is inviting me to lunch might not seem like anything to write home about, but if you know the turbulent history of our relationship, you will understand just how much of a big deal this is.

'Today. Now.' She replies. 'It's your day off, isn't it?'

Hitting the indicator, I pull over in a lay-by at the side of the road.

'Well, yes, but I already have plans for today.'

'Plans that can't be changed to suit your mother?'

A picture of Aidan jumps into my mind and I close my eyes, genuinely torn between seeing my mother and keeping my arrangement with him.

'Don't worry about it, Sadie.' Sounding highly disappointed, she sighs heavily. 'It was just on the off-chance, that's all. Just please remember I offered...'

Knowing that she's referring to her promise to build bridges with me, I feel my heart pang with guilt.

'What about this evening?' I ask hopefully. 'Are you free tonight?'

'Mick and I are going for dinner later, but I suppose I could call in for a coffee beforehand? Just the one though. You know what Mick is like when I'm late.'

I *do* know what Mick is like. I know all too well how deplorable my mother's partner is. Not that she would use that word herself. It's fair to say that our views on Mick are at opposite ends of the spectrum. She says dependable, I say manipulative. She says firm, I say controlling. She says bad back, I say bone idle. She says salt of the earth, I say money-grabbing, child-hating, greedy, awful man without an ounce of decency. The list is truly endless...

Not wanting to miss the opportunity to spend some time with my mum, I agree to a swift coffee and end the call. Mick isn't the only thing my mother and I don't agree on, but we have finally turned a corner and I desperately want to keep things on track.

Realising I'm going to be late, I put the car into gear and follow the curve of the road until I reach the turning for The Shepard. After taking the initial left, I almost miss the secluded dirt track that leads to the barn conversion where I am due to meet Aidan. Leaning closer to the windscreen, I grip the steering wheel as the uneven ground causes the car to shake. According to my sat nav the property should be at the end of this path, but I am starting to question if I have taken a wrong turn. The narrow road is surrounded by wiry bushes and brambles, making it extremely difficult to navigate my way through.

Just as I am going to give up and turn around, I spot a building hidden behind the trees up ahead. Creeping forward, I bring the car to a stop a few feet away from what I believe is the property we are here to view. The two cars that are parked on the gravel driveway signal that Aidan and Frankie are already here.

Leaving my handbag on the passenger seat, I step out of the car and look up at the barn dubiously. It's a lot bigger than it looked on the property listing, but it's also in a much worse condition. The brickwork is crumbling before my eyes and the few slates that are left on the roof are clinging on for dear life. Well, that might be a slight exaggeration, but to say that this place has been neglected would be the world's biggest understatement.

Coming to the conclusion that we've all had a wasted trip, I head inside to discover Aidan and who I presume to be Frankie, smiling from ear to ear.

'Hello...' I say cautiously, looking up as though expecting the ceiling to fall down at any moment.

'Sadie! This is Frankie.' Aidan says joyfully, stepping back as Frankie holds out her tanned hand. 'Frankie, Sadie.'

Flashing me a dazzling white smile, Frankie shakes my hand firmly.

'Nice to meet you, Sadie.'

'You too.' I reply, visibly jumping as a pigeon flies through the room.

'Well, I think we're pretty much done here...' Tossing her long hair over her shoulder, Frankie produces an information pack from her bag and hands it to Aidan. 'I have a few calls to make. Have another look around and I shall be in the car if you have any more questions.'

'That's great, thank you.' Not bothering to look at the documents, Aidan waits until the sound of her stilettos fades into silence before turning to me.

'So, what do you think?' He whispers, folding his arms. 'It's exactly what I was looking for.'

'It's a little... sorry?'

'I said, *it's exactly what I was looking for.*' Aidan repeats, taking a step towards me. 'Don't you like it?'

A little lost for words, I carefully follow him around the empty building and search for an adjective to use that isn't negative. Hiding behind him as he gives me a guided tour, I'm surprised to discover that the old barn is a fully-functioning home. It has an ancient, yet working bathroom, a retro kitchen that has seen better days and a few tired bedrooms that are bigger than most people's living rooms.

'Give me your honest opinion.' Aidan presses, positioning himself in front of me. 'Just tell me the truth.'

'It's certainly a project, that's for sure. It's clearly been well-loved, but it's also been left with more wear and tear than I would ever expect.' With a final look around the place, I decide to just hit him with it. 'To be honest, Aidan, this place is bloody knackered.'

'Like me...' Aidan replies, a slight smile playing on his lips. 'It's crying out for work, I realise that and if I am completely honest, it's probably a lot more of a project than I anticipated, but it's calling out to me. Do you know what I mean?'

Watching Aidan look up at the ceiling and smile fondly, I nod in response.

'I know exactly what you mean. I had the same feeling when I first stepped inside Blossom View. It just *consumed* me. Without going further than the hallway, I just knew it was meant for me. It might sound silly to you, but I could almost hear it calling my name.'

'It doesn't sound silly. I said the exact same thing to Frankie before you arrived, which is why I am buying it.'

'You are?' I gasp, my eyes widening in shock. 'You don't want to have a look at some other properties first?'

'I don't need to.' He says quietly, his voice lower than a whisper. 'When you have walked a mile in my shoes, you know what you want when you see it.'

There's a fuzzy silence, where neither of us knows what to say next and I attempt to fill it with a forced cough.

'Aidan?' Frankie shouts, the sound of her stilettoes echoing into the barn once more. 'Sorry to push you. It's just that I've got another viewing on this place in ten minutes.'

'No need.' Aidan replies, finally finding his voice. 'I'll take it.'

'Excellent!'

'Subject to survey, obviously.' He adds with a grin.

'*Obviously.*' Frankie repeats, her commission twinkling in her eyes. 'Well, I'll make a call and cancel the upcoming viewings. Congrats on your new home, Mr Wilder!'

Watching the two of them shake hands, I smile at Aidan as my stomach does cartwheels.

'Congratulations, Aidan. Welcome home...'

Chapter 6

'Here's to your new home!' Holding out my glass, I raise it in the air and smile at Aidan across the dining table. 'May it be a place where adventures begin, memories never end and most importantly, may it bring you a lifetime of happiness.'

'Thank you.' Clinking his champagne flute against mine, Aidan takes a sip of fizz and rests his elbows on the table. 'It feels so surreal to be purchasing another property. I was worried I wouldn't find anything... *ever*.'

I pull Mateo onto my lap and twirl his tail around my fingers as Aidan continues to speak.

'Once I sold the house back in Surrey, I didn't believe anywhere would ever feel like home again. It was like the ability to have somewhere that made me feel safe and secure died with Mel. That luxury was no longer mine.' Tipping back his head, Aidan sighs heavily and looks up at the ceiling. 'It's a funny thing, time, isn't it? You don't notice it until it's gone, yet it's the only thing that truly heals you. It's the only thing that allows you to recover and realise there *is* light at the end of the tunnel.'

'I completely agree. After my breakdown, I didn't believe I would ever be *me* again. The idea almost seemed laughable, but fast-forward twelve months and I don't recognise the frightened girl I was back then.'

'I could say the same about myself.' Aidan replies quietly. 'I still don't recognise the man who walked into your meeting that day, but I am slowly coming back. I can see it in the mirror and I can feel it inside. I'm not saying that I am completely healed, but I'm getting there...'

A commanding knock at the door interrupts his flow as we both look towards the window. Apologising to Aidan, I slip out from behind the table and walk down the hall. After quickly dusting a few crumbs off my blouse, I reach for the handle and pull open the door.

'Mum!' I manage, immediately remembering our arrangement. 'Hi...'

Dressed in her finest shift dress and matching bolero, she stands awkwardly on the doorstep, clutching what appears to be a bakery box to her chest.

'Why do you look so surprised to see me?' She asks, screwing up her nose. 'You didn't forget about our coffee date, did you?'

'No!' I exclaim, my pink cheeks revealing that I most certainly did. 'Well, yes, but, it's fine.'

'Okay...' Holding out the box, she waits for me to move aside before stepping into the cottage. 'Gosh! What a mess they have made in here!'

Scowling at a pile of broken tiles and rubble by the stairs, she shields her coat from a pair of rusty ladders and makes her way into the living room.

'Which firm are you using?' She asks, lifting up a delivery note and squinting at the writing.

'Erm, one from Prestwich. I can't remember the name.' Knowing she is going to stumble across Aidan at any moment, I clear my throat and try to make the introduction as smooth as possible. 'Mum...'

'They've left it a right state in here too, haven't they?' She grumbles, frowning as she inspects the bare plaster. 'I hope they're not taking advantage of you. These building firms are notorious for doing a shabby job when they know the client doesn't know a thing about...'

'Mum!' I interrupt abruptly, cutting her off mid-sentence.

Spinning around to face me, she raises her eyebrows and waits for me to explain myself.

'There's someone I would like you to meet.' Silently cursing myself for forgetting our coffee date, I lead her into the dining room and smile apologetically at Aidan. 'Mum, this is Aidan. Aidan, this is my mum, Linda.'

Immediately standing up, Aidan walks around the table and holds out his hand, completely unfazed.

'Oh!' She says dramatically, looking from me to Aidan and back again. 'Am I interrupting something?'

'Aidan is a friend from the support group.' I stammer. 'He's just agreed to purchase a property here, so we're toasting his new venture.'

Motioning for her to join us at the table, I grab another glass as she shakes Aidan's hand before taking a seat.

'It's lovely to meet you, Lisa.' Aidan says, oblivious to his error.

Freezing as I make my way back to the table, I notice my mum's smile drop as she cautiously sits down opposite Aidan.

'It's *Linda*, but thank you, *Aidan*, is lovely to meet you, too.' She replies, placing her handbag as far away from Mateo as possible. 'You should have said if you had plans tonight, Sadie. I feel terrible for intruding on your evening.'

Shaking off her apology, I take a big gulp from my glass. The truth is, once I arrived at the barn conversion earlier, all thoughts of our coffee date completely vanished. I'm ashamed to admit the only thing on my mind was celebrating Aidan's monumental milestone.

'So, what do you think of the kitchen?' Aidan asks, obviously trying to rectify the awkwardness with idle chit-chat. 'It's really coming along, isn't it?'

Begrudgingly pushing herself up, my mum pops her head into the kitchen and has a brief look around. I hold my breath at the sound of her heels clacking on the concrete floor as she inspects the ongoing transformation.

'They're certainly not tidy workers, are they?' She remarks, coming back into the dining room with a fundraiser leaflet in her hand. 'What's this?'

'Oh, it's the annual Anxiety Anonymous fundraiser.' Trying to stop Mateo from pawing her expensive handbag, I distract him with one of his toys. 'Do you want to come along?'

'When is it?'

'A week on Sunday.' Taking the leaflet from her, I pass it across the table to Aidan. 'We're looking for people to get involved with cake stalls, prizes for the tombola and so forth.'

'Sounds great!' Aidan says encouragingly. 'Anxiety Anonymous pretty much saved my life. I'd love to get involved.'

'Fantastic! How about you, Mum?'

'I'll... I'll try and pop down.' She manages eventually, feigning interest. 'Maybe I could get Mick to do some of his magic tricks for the kids.'

Resisting the urge to tell her that the last thing children at a fundraiser want is to be subjected to Mick's boozy David Blaine act, I nod along silently.

'Tickets are available from the Anxiety Anonymous website and from the support groups.' I explain, starting to feel excited about the event. 'It should be a lovely day for the village and a great opportunity to raise awareness of such an important subject.'

'I'm sure it will be.' Giving Mateo a dubious glance, my mum hauls her handbag onto her shoulder. 'Anyway, I better get going. Enjoy your evening and I'll give you a call tomorrow. Aidan, it was nice to meet you. Congratulations on your new home.'

'Thank you, Linda. I'll see you at the fundraiser.'

Following her to the door, I give her a brief hug as she steps outside and digs her car keys out of her bag.

'I'm so sorry about tonight, Mum.' I whisper, watching her walk down the path and jump into her car. 'We'll reschedule. Just let me know when you're free.'

Waiting until she starts the engine and disappears down the lane, I close the door with my hip and retreat to the dining room.

'I'm so sorry about that.' I apologise, holding my head in my hands. 'I totally forgot I had invited her over here tonight...'

'Don't be sorry.' Aidan cuts in, picking up the empty champagne bottle and placing it on the kitchen counter. 'She seems lovely.'

'She's not lovely.' Smiling back at him, I roll my eyes and laugh lightly. 'She's cold, disapproving, condescending and critical of my every move, but she's my mum.'

Choosing to reply with nothing more than a wry smile, Aidan leans against the sink and folds his arms.

'What's in the box?' He asks.

'I have no idea.' Pulling the pink box towards me, I flip back the lid and feel my heart pang. 'They're cakes. Vanilla slices, to be exact.'

Staring up at me are two pristine mille-feuilles. Perfectly iced and cut into identical rectangles, the humble cakes fill me with nostalgic memories. To anyone else these are simply a couple of cute cakes, but to me they represent so much more. It's no secret that my mother and I have a strained relationship now, but things weren't always this way. Back when I was a child, before the money and the move to Cheshire, there was one little thing that brought my mum and I together.

Every Friday, my mum would collect me from school with two mille-feuilles from the posh bakery on our neighbouring estate. Those thirty minutes we would spend together used to make eight-year-old me so deliriously happy. Our weekly pit stops at the park were one of the only times I felt really connected to my mum. In that half an hour, when we sat on the same bench, eating the same fancy cakes, my mum wasn't a stressed worker or a frustrated woman trying to make ends meet. She was simply my mother and I loved her for it.

A lump forms in the back of my throat and I suddenly feel incredibly guilty for forgetting about our coffee date. She *is* trying to build bridges with me. She *is* making an effort. I have just been too blind to see it.

'Those look amazing.' Aidan remarks, peering into the box. 'They're almost too pretty to eat.'

'Aren't they just...' Tearing off the lid, I hold out the box and smile. 'Here, try one.'

'Are you sure?' He asks, his hand hovering above the cakes.

'Absolutely positive.'

Watching Aidan as he dives in, I recognise the same smile on his face that these used to bring me as a child. The wide eyes, the swooning expression and the nod of appreciation after the very first bite. It would appear that they still have their magic.

'Good?' I ask, already knowing the answer.

'Incredible.'

They say you can't have your cake and eat it too, but as with all things in life, there are *always* exceptions to the rule...

Chapter 7

After my mum left last night, Aidan and I chatted until the early hours about his plans for the future, how he envisages the barn renovations and how happy Mel would be for him. The last subject is the one which led us past midnight. Watching Aidan talk about his late wife and not be wrought with grief was the highlight of my night. He's finally remembering the good times he shared with Mel, without kicking himself for daring to believe in a future without her.

If you have ever experienced grief first-hand, you will know that the grieving process is like the layers of an onion. Each phase leads to something that feels exactly the same as the stage before, but the grief becomes smaller with each layer you peel back. Last night felt like the final layer being torn off. It was the last piece of the puzzle Aidan needed to know that he has made the right decision to start his life again here. He might not ever be the same man he was before he lost his wife, but Aidan's put himself back together in a way Mel would be proud of.

My late-night chat with Aidan is incidentally why I am running so late for work this morning. I should have left to host the Anxiety Anonymous meeting ten minutes ago and if I'm any later, there won't be a support group for me to arrive to. Trying to shake all thoughts of Aidan to the back of my mind, I dodge the seemingly-permanent pile of rubble in the hall and head into the kitchen. Not bothering to look for a glass, I grab the bottle of milk from the fridge and take a big gulp.

'Excuse me, love!'

Spinning around, my eyes widen when I discover one of the builders is waiting by the kitchen door.

'Would it be alright if I wash my hands in here? This plaster's a nightmare to get off.'

'Yes, of course.' Quickly wiping my mouth and placing the bottle back into the fridge, I pass him a tea towel.

Leaving him to use the sink, I start to walk away and stop when I realise it's the same builder I thought I recognised earlier in the week. Allowing curiosity to get the better of me, I take a few steps back and watch him washing his hands at the basin. Wearing a pair of paint-stained overalls and a pair of Timberland boots, he looks just like any of the other builders that have been swarming around here lately.

'How are you getting on?' I ask, leaning against the wall.

Giving me a cursory glance over his shoulder, he nods and coughs into his sleeve.

'Yeah, it's coming along nicely. Still got quite a way to go, but so far so good.'

'That's a strong accent.' I remark, smiling as he dries his hands. 'I'm guessing you're not local?'

'Me? You've got to be joking!' Letting out a scoff, the builder laughs loudly and shakes his head. 'I'm from Manchester, love. Born and bred.'

'Me too, originally.'

'Are you really?' He replies, turning around to face me for the first time. 'How did you end up down here then?'

Deciding he doesn't need to hear about my mum's infamous lottery win, I shrug my shoulders.

'It's a long story...'

'Well, you certainly landed on your feet, didn't you? My missus would love to live down here. She's always watching that housewife show. Do you know the one? Footballers and fancy restaurants...'

Nodding along as he speaks, I study his face and try to think where I have seen those eyes before. The thick beard is acting like a disguise, shielding the majority of his features with a blanket of peppered grey, but those green eyes are calling out to me.

'She's always going on about this... *Golden Triangle* is our Angela. She'd cut her arm off to be one of those housewives. Last year, she made me drive down that Macclesfield Road after seeing it on the tele. She just wanted to have a look at the big houses. Couldn't bloody help herself.' Rubbing his extremely-tanned face, he sighs and shakes his head. 'It's a different world here to where I live. A different world entirely...'

My phone pings in my hand, reminding me there's a whole room of people waiting for me in Wilmslow.

'Well, I won't keep you from your work...' Realising I don't know his name, I bite my lip and hope that he fills in the blank.

'Gavin.' He offers, holding out a weather-beaten hand. 'But everyone calls me Gav.'

Taking his hand in mine, I give his familiar eyes a final stare.

'I'm Sadie.'

Gav. Gavin. Gavin. Gavin. Those eyes. That name.

'Where did you say you were from again, Gavin?' I ask, holding my breath as I wait for his reply.

'Middleton, love. You probably won't know it.'

Feeling my stomach drop to the floor, I hold on to the wall to steady myself. Oh, I know it alright. I know the place, I know the name and I know those eyes. The beard might be new, as is the intense tan, but there's no mistaking who this man is now...

'You alright, love? You look a bit peaky.'

Struggling to regain the use of my tongue, I try to stop my racing heart. How did I not see it until now? How has he been here all this time without me realising who he is? How could I possibly forget? He looks very different to how he did the first and only time I laid eyes on him, but it's definitely him.

Gav. Gavin. Gavin Gastrell. My biological father.

'Erm... yes... I'm... I'm fine.' Forcing myself to smile, I try to keep breathing normally. 'I just... remembered something I had to do.'

'Ah...' Folding the used tea towel neatly, he places it on the counter and points to the fundraiser leaflet on the fridge. 'This looks fun. I don't know much about mental health stuff myself, but these things are always entertaining, aren't they?'

He doesn't know who I am. Of course, he doesn't. He didn't recognise me a year ago when I pulled up outside his home, so why would he recognise me now? He has no idea that his estranged daughter came to find him, because I never introduced myself. I didn't want or need to. I simply had an urge to see him for myself. I just needed to come face-to-face with the man who made me and look him in the eyes...

'Can anyone attend this, or do you have to be part of the Cheshire Set?' He continues, completely oblivious to my impending panic attack. 'The missus would be made up if I brought her down here, as would the kids.'

'Kids?' I stammer, thinking back to the two children I saw heading into his house on that fateful day. 'You... you have kids?'

'Yeah. Two. Well, they're not really kids anymore. Our Paige is twenty-one and Mitch is sixteen, sorry, seventeen. He was seventeen just last week.'

He has other children. I suspected as much. Paige and Mitch. Mitch and Paige. My half-siblings.

'Demanding a car now. That's where all my wages will be going, getting him a driving licence. I shouldn't complain though. Not being a taxi service anymore will be a welcome change. Mind you, if he takes after his mother, Angela, it's the other drivers I feel sorry for...'

I laugh along, amazed by my ability to cover my shock with a forced giggle.

'Here they are...' Digging a set of keys out of his pocket, he points to a faded picture in a plastic keyring. 'Lights of my life, apples of my eye, holes in my bloody pockets...'

Taking the keys, I hold the photograph close to my face. Standing in front of the Cinderella Castle wearing iconic Mickey Mouse ears, Paige, Mitch, Gavin and who I presume to be Angela, beam proudly for the camera. Their skin is sun-kissed and their smiles are real. They look the image of family togetherness. The kind of family I have always longed for.

'Is it just the two?' I ask, unable to take my eyes off the photograph. 'Kids, I mean.'

'Oh, yes. Twos enough for anyone.' He jokes, taking the keys back. 'Double trouble, I say. Twice the cost and twice the worry. I'll always worry about them, no matter how old they are. It's a dad's job, isn't it?'

'It sure is...' A lump forms in my throat and I bite my lip in a bid to expel it.

'Anyway, I better get back to work.' He says with a grin. 'You don't pay us to stand around gabbing, do you?'

Shaking my head, I desperately try to think of something to say to stop him from leaving.

'Would you mind if I took this?' He asks, pointing to the fundraiser leaflet. 'Be something to make the wife smile when I get home.'

'Not, not at all.' I stammer in response. 'Tickets are available on the website.'

'Great stuff. I'll have to get our Mitch to do that. I don't do well with computers.' Tucking the leaflet into his back pocket, he offers me a nod and slips out into the garden. 'You have a great day, love!'

Staring at the place where he once stood, I try to process what just happened. Gavin Gastrell. My dad. The human who made me. He's actually in my home, yet he still has absolutely no idea who I am.

Waiting until my heart rate returns to its usual rhythm, I calmly reach for my handbag and walk out of the front door, without daring to look back...

* * *

I've been waiting in my car outside the Anxiety Anonymous building for the last ten minutes, but I haven't moved a muscle. The entire drive over here has been clouded in a strange fuzz. The first and last time I saw Gavin, I cried myself to sleep. I felt a part of me that was missing for so long become even bigger than it was before. The dad-shaped hole inside me wasn't filled with love as I expected, it was accentuated and made impossible to ignore. This time, however, I couldn't feel more different to how I did back then.

Oddly, once the initial panic subsided, I felt nothing. Literally nothing at all. Apart from running incredibly late, today feels no different to any other. How? How can my reaction be so dissimilar? I am the same person. He is the same man. If anything, I should be even more shocked than I was the first time. I have siblings. I am a biological part of his family, whether he knows it or not.

My calmness is unnerving me slightly as I stare at the Anxiety Anonymous building in silence, but before I can commit another moment to analysing my absurd reaction, the sight of Alec walking out of the door makes me snap to attention.

Jumping out of the driver's seat, I grab my handbag and run after him.

'Alec!' I yell. 'I'm so sorry I'm late. I had a little... family trouble.'

'Is everything okay?' He asks, sounding very concerned. 'A few of the others have already left. They presumed you weren't coming...'

'Everything's fine, thanks for asking. It's just been one of those mornings.' Leading the way into the meeting room, I offer the remaining attendees an apologetic smile. 'So sorry, guys. I do apologise for keeping you all waiting. I was just saying to Alec, it's been one hell of a morning.'

A chorus of understanding mumbles come back at me as I shake off my jacket and pull the fundraiser leaflets out of my handbag.

'Okay. I realise we're already short for time, but before we start I just need a few moments to tell you all about the annual Anxiety Anonymous fundraiser...'

As I continue to fill people in on the charity's upcoming event, I take in the dozen smiling faces that are beaming back at me. Just as I expected, almost everyone is keen to get involved in the action. With people offering to bake cookies, donate pieces to the tombola and even help out with the running of the show, it seems the fundraiser is a huge success before it has even started.

'I could bring a few hampers from the farm.' Yvette offers, raising her hand in the air. 'We supply luxury gift baskets of organic produce to a farm shop in Knutsford. I wouldn't mind donating a few to the tombola.'

'That would be great, Yvette. Thank you.' I reply gratefully. 'Any and all donations will be greatly appreciated.'

'Maybe you could do a motivational speech.' Alec says, slipping a leaflet into his briefcase. 'You know, as someone who has been through anxiety and beat it. After all, it's not just about raising money, it's about raising awareness.'

Opening my mouth to decline, I close it again when Yvette jumps on the bandwagon.

'That's a fantastic idea! As someone who is new to learning about mental health, I know I would find it extremely useful.' Yvette says encouragingly, as the rest of the people in the room nod along. 'You're in a unique position in that you have crossed the bridge from sufferer to counsellor. I'm sure lots of people would be very interested in hearing what you have to say.'

My cheeks blush and I fidget with my hands uncomfortably.

'I'm not over the bridge completely. I do still have the odd wobble here and there...'

'Nonsense!' Alec interrupts. 'Don't put yourself down. What you have achieved is incredible. You've done amazingly well! Hasn't she, guys?'

A round of applause echoes around the room and I find myself succumbing to their praise.

'Alright! If you think it will help, I will say a few words at the fundraiser.' Smiling at Alec as he shoots me the thumbs-up sign, I finally pull out a chair and take my seat. 'Now, let's get this meeting started...'

Chapter 8

Slipping my shoulders beneath the surface of the water, I allow my eyes to close and sigh heavily. The warmth of the water soothes my aching body as I tip back my head and look up at the old ceiling above me. It's not even dark outside, but I'm already craving the sanctuary of my bed. Today has been bizarre, to say the least, but despite my shock at discovering Gavin Gastrell in my kitchen this morning, I've managed to go about my daily tasks without giving it a second thought. It's almost as though it didn't really happen, or it happened in a dreamworld that I'm expecting to wake up from at any moment.

Only, it isn't a dream, is it? He *was* here today and he will be here tomorrow and every day after that until the job is done. I think back to the moment I realised his true identity and ask myself why I didn't say something. Why I didn't press him more. Why I didn't react in the way I thought I would. *Do you know a woman named Linda Valentine? Did you live on the Litchfield estate? Did you walk out on a young woman who fell pregnant with your child and leave her to raise the baby alone?*

Strangely, I feel more powerful not revealing myself. To him or to anyone, for that matter. The fact that I know and he doesn't makes me feel in control of the situation. If it is at all possible for *anyone* to be in charge of a situation like this. Just who does hold the cards? Me? Him? My mum? An image of my mum pops into my mind and I wonder what she would say if she knew he'd been here. The one and only time I asked about my biological father was a moment I shall remember forever and not in a good way.

Closing my eyes, I shuffle further down the tub and allow the ends of my hair to soak through. Water rushes into my ears, blocking out the rest of the world as I zone in on my heartbeat and focus on the steady rhythm. Maybe Gavin Gastrell coming back into my life is a sign. Maybe him being here is fate's way of bringing us together and giving me an opportunity to have the father figure I've always longed for.

My heart rate increases as I picture myself telling him who I am. I imagine his face breaking into a smile. His green eyes, which are identical to mine, lighting up with joy. I feel his arms wrap around me as we embrace one another warmly. I envisage being introduced to his wife, my half-siblings and the rest of his extended family. Gavin Gastrell. Angela Gastrell. Paige Gastrell. Mitch Gastrell. Sadie Gastrell.

If only. I'm old enough to know that life isn't a movie and things don't always have the happy ending we desire. Mentally rewinding the scene, I start over and feel my new-found happiness quickly ebb away. I picture his face falling as the words *you're my dad* tumble out of my mouth. I see his eyes darken, in a way mine never have. I feel him brush past me as he flees Blossom View, never to return again. I picture him crossing the road with his family, desperate for them to never know who I am. Gavin Gastrell. Angela Gastrell. Paige Gastrell. Mitch Gastrell. Sadie Valentine.

Peeling open my eyes, I push myself into a sitting position and wrap my arms around my legs. My wet hair clings to my body as I stare into the glistening bubbles, succumbing to the overwhelming sadness that is washing over me. It could go one of two ways. The outcome of telling him would rest on the flip of a coin. Good or bad. Positive or negative. Heads or tails. Dad or just a humble builder...

Resting my chin on my knees, I reach for a towel as my phone rings from the windowsill beside me. Ruby's name flashes on the screen and I quickly rearrange my bubbles before hitting the green button. Almost immediately, the black monitor springs to life and Ruby's face appears before me.

'Sadie? Hello? Can you see me, Sadie?'

The sound of my good friend's voice turns my frown upside down as I nod my head in response.

'Yes, I can see you.'

'Oh, there you are!' She cheers, waving at the screen manically. 'Are you in the bath?'

'Yes.' I confess, holding the phone a little higher. 'It's been a long day...'

Ruby frowns at the camera and brushes her windswept hair out of her face.

'Anything you want to talk about?'

I bite my lip as I debate telling Ruby about this morning's events, but the truth is, I really don't want to discuss it. Not with Ruby. Not with anyone.

'Not really.' I reply honestly. 'How are you? How are things going over there?'

'I'm good.' Clumsily jumping into a hammock, Ruby sways back and forth gently. 'We moved islands this morning and we're now in... *Saint Lucia!'*

Turning the screen around to reveal the flag of Saint Lucia billowing in the breeze, she offers me a view of a beautiful mountain in the distance.

'And it's just as spectacular as the rest.' She gushes, her eyes sparkling as she speaks. 'I think this one could be my favourite...'

My spirits lift as I listen to Ruby's tales of fun in the Caribbean sun. Witnessing her giggle like the carefree teenager she was always meant to be is exactly what the doctor ordered.

'It's so great to hear that you're having a great time!' I reply, blowing a cluster of bubbles off my shoulder. 'You will be pleased to know your mum was at the Anxiety Anonymous meeting again today.'

'She was?' She asks, shielding her eyes from the sun.

'Yes. She's made a massive effort to integrate herself into the group. I think you will be very surprised at the change in her when you return.'

'*If* I return!' Ruby corrects teasingly.

'Oh, come on! You can't stay away from Alderley forever...'

'I'm only joking.' She replies with a smile. 'As beautiful as the Caribbean is, I must confess to feeling a little homesick. Not enough to come back though. Not yet, anyway...'

With Ruby's history of anxiety, I've been waiting for her to throw in the towel and declare she was jumping on the next flight home, but thankfully, she is taking to her working vacation like a duck to water and I couldn't be prouder if I tried.

'Well, I better let you go and dry off.' Stepping out of the hammock, she stretches out her arms and points to a little hut in the distance. 'There's a rum punch with my name on it, but I'm only a phone call away if you need me…'

After saying our goodbyes, I end the call and reach for a towel, just in time to hear a knock at the door. Quickly wrapping myself in my dressing gown, I curse under my breath and race down the stairs. This is the second time I have been caught short by visitors lately and it's starting to become an annoying habit.

Pressing my nose against the glass, I smile as I spot Aldo on the doorstep, wine bottle in hand.

'Hi!' I exclaim, kissing his cheek as he steps inside the cottage. 'What are you doing here?'

'Since when do I need a reason?' Pressing the cold bottle of fizz against my bare neck, he laughs when I squeal. 'Can't a guy just call on his best friend to put the world to rights anymore?'

Looking at the ice-cold bottle in his hand, I crack a smile and allow the door to close behind him.

'Where's fleabag?' He asks, shaking off his leather jacket and tossing it onto the couch carelessly.

'If you're referring to Mateo, he's probably still in the bathroom playing with the rug.' Taking the bottle from him, I grab two glasses from the kitchen. 'And if you could refrain from referring to him as *fleabag* it would be greatly appreciated.'

Choosing to ignore my request, Aldo follows me into the kitchen and runs his hands over the sparkling new counters.

'They're doing a great job in here. You'll have to give me their card.'

My smile falters at the mention of the building work and I try to pretend I haven't heard him.

'So, what brings you here?' I ask. 'You never just call in anymore.'

'Why are you changing the subject?' Aldo retorts quickly, narrowing his eyes.

'I'm not!' Blood rushes to my cheeks and I focus on filling the glasses with crisp bubbles.

'You *are* happy with the work, aren't you?'

'Of course, I'm happy. They're doing a great job. You said so yourself...' I motion around the kitchen and clink my glass against his. 'So, why are you really here?'

Reluctantly letting the subject drop as Mateo pads into the kitchen, Aldo groans loudly.

'I don't know. I guess I just needed to get out for a few hours.'

'Okay...' Leading the way into the living room, I wait for Mateo to follow us inside before closing the door. 'What's with the long face? Isn't Edward home tomorrow?'

'Yup...' He replies, kicking off his shoes and sprawling out on the couch like a teenager. 'He sure is.'

My BFF senses go into overdrive as I mimic his actions and take a seat opposite him.

'You don't sound exactly thrilled about that.'

'I *am* thrilled about it. Overjoyed, in fact.'

Zoning in on my dear friend's face, I try to work out what's troubling him. His blue eyes just aren't glittering the way they usually do.

'What's going on?' I press, shuffling closer to him.

Not responding, Aldo runs his fingers through his hair and stares into his glass.

'I don't know.' He eventually mumbles. 'I've just been feeling a little... *funny* lately.'

'What kind of funny?'

Taking a big swig from his glass, Aldo rubs his new inking with a forlorn look on his face.

'Shirley, what does anxiety feel like?'

A little taken aback, I place my own drink on the coffee table and rest my hands in my lap.

'Well, anxiety feels different for everyone, but for me, anxiety is a constant sense of dread in the pit of my stomach. It's a feeling of fear, trepidation and dismay that comes from no explicable place. Anxiety makes my heart race, my palms sweat and my head throb with panic. The nausea is probably my worse symptom. The over-whelming sickness that would hit me the second I opened my eyes every morning and refused to leave was the part I found the hardest. It almost made me believe I was *physically* ill. Anxiety, Aldo, is quite simply awful...' Recognising I've gone off on a tangent, I frown at Aldo in confusion. 'Why do you ask?'

'It's just... it's just that, this time apart from Edward has made me fall back in love with myself again.' He admits honestly. 'I've been able to do the things I wanted to do without having to seek someone else's approval first. I've had a chance to rediscover what I love and forget about interior design, mortgages, trips to Ikea and adoption...'

'Adoption?' I repeat, feeling my jaw drop open. 'Since when has adoption been on the cards?'

'Edward's fallen in love with a stray dog in Los Angeles and he wants to fly her back with him.'

'Oh...' Resting my chin in the palm of my hand, I try to get the conversation back on track. 'Just to be clear, you're saying that you've had too much fun drinking tequila and dancing on tables while Edward's been away?'

'No! Not at all. I've hardly been away from the salon...'

'Aldo, Patrick told me you stumbled out of Precious at two in the morning a few days back.'

'Okay, I might have let my hair down a little bit, but that really isn't what this is about.' Pushing himself into a sitting position, Aldo pulls a cushion onto his lap. 'The idea of Edward *not* coming back fills me with a happiness I can't quite explain.'

'And the idea of him coming home?'

Pausing before he answers, Aldo considers my question carefully.

'The idea of him coming back fills me with all of those awful things you just said.'

Completely lost for words, I take Aldo's hand in mine and squeeze it tightly. The thought of Aldo feeling so low makes my heart ache.

'Aldo, you don't need me to tell you that you shouldn't be in a relationship if it isn't making you happy.' I say gently. 'A relationship should bring out the best version of you, not the worst.'

'That's exactly how I feel right now. The worst version of me.' Aldo says with a sad smile. 'Since Edward told me he was coming home, I've felt like the life has been battered out of me. I feel completely deflated. The truth is, I just don't want to be with him anymore.'

Raising my eyebrows at his revelation, I desperately search for the correct thing to say.

'He's going to be devastated.' Aldo whispers, before I can respond. 'He's talking about marriage, adoption and everything that comes with it. How am I going to tell him that it's over?'

'Are you absolutely sure there's no future with Edward?' I ask. 'Like, one hundred and ten percent?'

Slowly nodding, Aldo drains the contents of his glass in one swift gulp.

'I knew it was over a long time ago, but I didn't want to admit to myself.'

'Then you're just going to have to sit him down and tell him.' I say seriously. 'As much as I love Edward, you can't stay with him if your heart isn't in it. You *both* deserve to be happy.'

We lock eyes and for the first time I notice just how much this situation with Edward is hurting him. In all the years that Aldo and I have been friends, I can count on one hand the number of times he has opened up to me. Not being one to talk about his feelings, the fact that he's even told me about this means it's cutting him pretty deeply.

Just as I'm about to let him know he can always come to me with anything that's bothering him, Aldo places his empty glass on the coffee table and reaches behind him. Scowling as he feels around beneath the cushions, he pulls out a scarf and holds it in the air using the tips of his fingers.

'What the hell is this?' He asks, grimacing at the chequered scarf in disgust. 'What year is it? 2002?'

Immediately recognising the offending article as belonging to Aidan, I reach out and take the scarf from Aldo.

'Sorry, it's... mine.' I lie, instantly feeling bad for lying to him.

'Since when do you wear Burberry?' Aldo says suspiciously, taking my glass into the kitchen for a refill.

Not wanting to lie to him again, I ignore the question and trace his steps across the dining room. With Mateo by my feet, I hop onto the counter and watch Aldo expertly fill our glasses with a flourish. His lips purse as he concentrates on making sure both glasses are identical, before wiping a splash of fizz from the counter. Typical Aldo, forever the perfectionist.

'Why are you looking at me like that?' He asks, reaching into the fridge and dropping a couple of edible flowers into the glasses.

'No reason.' Pulling him towards me, I grab Mateo from the floor and envelope them both in a huge bear hug.

'Just know that regardless of what happens with Edward, I love you, Aldo Cristiano Taylor and fleabag does, too...'

OUR FREEDOM IS CONFINED BY THE WALLS WE BUILD OURSELVES.

Chapter 9

'One of the most difficult aspects of anxiety to understand is often the physical symptoms it can present itself in. Those who have never been affected by anxiety probably won't be aware of just how strong these symptoms can be.' I explain, looking around the circle of people as I address the support group. 'As we have just heard from Jane, palpitations can be an extremely frightening thing to experience. Being sufferers of anxiety, many of us will have experienced panic attacks first-hand. While we might not be in control of the physical symptoms anxiety inflicts on us, we *are* in control of how we respond to them.'

Pausing to take a deep breath, I twist my ring around my finger and focus on the lady at the far end of the circle.

'To answer your question, Jane, the first step to taking control of a panic attack is recognising you're having one. When a panic attack hits, it's very easy to allow the panic to take over and in doing that you're feeding its power. The quicker you realise that you have the tools in yourself to stop the panic in its tracks, the quicker you can take back control over your body. Cognitive behavioural therapies are just one of the ways that have been proven to be very successful in handling the way we deal with panic attacks.'

Nodding along, Janie fidgets in her seat and cracks her knuckles nervously.

'I just feel like such a failure for allowing my anxiety to affect me like this.' She says quietly, as everyone in the room fixes their gaze on her. 'In every other aspect of my life, I am completely in control. How can I run a multinational company, yet I let this *thing* control my happiness? I just don't understand it. I don't understand it at all.'

'Anxiety and depression affect people from all walks of life.' I explain regretfully. 'It doesn't matter whether you're male or female, young or old, career-driven or laid-back. I'm afraid there aren't any mitigating circumstances. It's important to understand that suffering from anxiety does not make you weak. It makes you human.'

Jane sighs sadly as the rest of the group mumble in agreement.

'However, almost everyone can achieve positive results with CBT. I can testify to its credibility from my own personal experience. In fact, I still rely on CBT today.' Pointing to Alec, I reach over to the information stand and pass a leaflet to Jane. 'Alec, you have been using CBT for a while now, haven't you?'

'I have.' He replies, turning in his seat to face Jane. 'It's not an overnight success story. It takes a while to get into the swing of things, but I have...'

Listening to Alec as he tells Jane about his success with CBT, I smile in surprise as I notice my mum peering through the window. Raising my eyebrows, I nod back at her as she signals that she will wait outside.

A discreet glance at the clock tells me that the meeting has run over and I clap my hands together to gain everyone's attention.

'I think that concludes our meeting for today. As usual, feel free to stay behind and enjoy the complimentary coffees and I shall see you all very soon!'

A quick round of applause erupts as I say my goodbyes and gather my belongings. Not wanting to keep my mum waiting, I quickly wave to Yvette before making my way outside.

'Hello!' I grin, digging my sunglasses out of my handbag. 'What brings you here?'

Curling her red lips into half a smile, my mum slips her hands into her pockets tensely.

'Well, since you double-booked me the other day, I thought it might be nice to have our coffee date now.' She says, reaching into a glossy bag and producing a box identical to the one she brought to Blossom View a couple of days ago.

Knowing without opening it that it will contain two vanilla slices, I grin at the pink box happily.

'Did you go all the way back to The Cupcake Corner for these?'

'Twice.' She replies, almost haughtily. 'I went all the way back for the first set, too.'

'That's so kind of you, Mum.' Touched by her thoughtful gesture, I give her a brief hug. 'Thank you.'

'Where's your car?' Ignoring my gratitude, she shields her eyes from the sun and scours the car park.

'I walked.' I explain. 'With it being such a wonderful day, I thought I would make the most of it.'

She looks down at her heels dubiously and purses her lips.

'We can get a cab back, if you want?' I offer, knowing how much she hates any form of exercise that doesn't involve her hunky personal trainer and a G&T at the end.

'No, a walk would be nice...'

Falling into step next to me, she takes a deep breath before exhaling deeply. Not having spent time alone with my mother for so long, I don't really know what to say to her. It's not as though we have many common interests, a shared love for her partner or joint activities we engage in. As much as I hate to admit it, my mum has almost become a stranger to me.

'Dora was still there.' She says suddenly, breaking the silence as we cross the street.

'Sorry?'

'Dora.' She repeats slowly. 'From the bakery.'

'No!' I exclaim. 'She can't possibly still be there. She was ancient when I was eight!'

'Cheeky.'

'Oh, come on! How old must she be now?'

'I have no idea. One hundred and eighty?'

Erupting into giggles, we crease over with laughter and continue on our way.

'I miss those days...' She says quietly, a wistful expression on her face.

'You do?' Giving her a sideways glance, I slow down my pace.

'Very much so. Life was simpler back then. Yes, things were... *hard* at times, but it was just you and me. The two of us against the world. Battling against the odds and triumphing every time...'

For the past five years, my mum and I haven't really said more than hi and bye to one another. To hear her speak about my upbringing is something so alien to me. I don't quite know how to react to it.

'It was a time I look back on fondly.' She continues. 'Don't you?'

Not wanting to ruin her rose-tinted memories of our time back on the estate, I smile back at her in silence. The truth is, the days before Mick came onto the scene *were* the best days of my life. Well, if you discount the vile school bullies, the streets that weren't safe to walk around after dark and the neighbours from hell who made our lives a living nightmare. Not having Mick around might have been a plus, but the rest of our existence back there was frankly dreadful.

'I have to admit, it's a little rough around the edges these days. The estate, that is.' She confesses, as we approach the cottage. 'The place has gone really downhill, but the park is still there and the bench we used to eat our cakes on is still in one piece. Just about, anyway.'

'Maybe we should go back there one time.' I muse. 'You know, for old times' sake.'

'I don't know about that, Sadie. There's no point revisiting old memories. It's best to recreate them here. As far as I am concerned, the past should remain in the past...'

My stomach flips as I spot a cluster of vans outside Blossom View up ahead and I visibly gulp. What are they still doing here? They should be gone by now. It's six o'clock. Not a day has passed where they haven't packed away their tools and hit the road before the clock hit four.

Hearing laughter float out of the vans, my ears start to ring with adrenaline. What if Gavin is here? What if the man my mother advised me to stay well away from is in my home as we speak, just a few feet away…

'Hiya, Sadie!' Jason shouts, from his position at the back of one of the vans. 'I'm just finishing up here. The rest of the lads have gone, but I'll be out of your hair in ten minutes.'

'No problem.' I reply, relieved to hear the cottage is a Gavin-free zone. 'Thanks, Jason.'

Leaving him to pack away his tools, I lead the way into Blossom View and hang my cardigan on the coat stand.

'So, shall we have these cakes then?' I say to my mum, who is looking around the cottage as though a bomb has hit it. 'We could eat them in the garden, if you like? We might as well make the most of this beautiful weather.'

Responding with a simple nod of the head, she continues to inspect the building work with the same disdain she had the last time she was here. Allowing her to critique my choice of cabinets, the quality of the craftsmanship and everything in between, I head into the living room and place the cakes on the coffee table.

'I don't suppose you fancy a glass of fizz with these, do you?' I shout over my shoulder. 'I know it's a bit early, but I've got half a bottle left over that Aldo brought.'

Twisting my hair into a bun at the nape of my neck, I push back the drapes to allow some light to flood into the cottage.

'Mum?' I repeat. 'Should we have some bubbles?'

Heading into the dining room to see what's keeping her, I push open the door to the kitchen and feel my stomach sink to the ground. At opposite ends of the room, Gavin Gastrell and my mum stare at one another looking equally as sickened. He's here. He's really here. They've come face-to-face and there's absolutely nothing I can do to stop it.

Their faces are ashen and their eyes are wide with shock. It's as though time has stopped still. It's as though the world has stopped spinning. It's as though... it's as though I'm not even in the room with them.

'Hi, Gavin.' I say cautiously, trying my hardest to act like I can't sense the unbearable atmosphere. 'This is my mum, Linda.'

'Your... your *mum?*' He echoes, his face visibly paling as he stares at her in sheer disbelief.

Managing a slight nod of the head, I glance at my mum and notice her chest rise and fall at an alarming rate. This is it. This is the moment where he discovers my true identity. He looks sick, *she* looks sick, but neither of them knows that I know.

'Mum, this is Gavin.' I say quietly, completely unaware why I am still talking. 'He's part of the team who are working on the cottage.'

Standing between my mother and the man who I know as my father, I feel the hairs on the back of my neck stand on end. I can't take this much longer. I am going to have to say something. I should just come out with it and tell them everything I know. I should just get it over with, right here, right now...

'You ready, Gav?' Jason asks, popping his head into the kitchen and grinning broadly.

Responding with nothing but complete silence, Gavin slips a spanner into his tool belt and brushes past my mum.

'See you tomorrow, love!' Jason says sunnily. 'Have a good evening!'

Losing the ability to speak, I stare at the place where Gavin once stood and feel my blood run cold. For the first time in my life, my mum and dad have been in the same room together. Just the three of us. The three people who should make up the typical nuclear family are together at last. Only, the reality isn't as nice as that sounds, is it? The truth is far ickier. A man who ran out on his pregnant teenage girlfriend and a woman who has, until recently, put her vile boyfriend before her only child. Not quite the pretty picture I was painting.

Looking at my mum out of the corner of my eye, my skin prickles as I see she appears rocked to the core. When I first dared to ask about my dad, she screamed the house down and promptly burst into hysterics, so her prolonged silence is making me increasingly uncomfortable. The fact of the matter remains, she has no idea that I know who Gavin is. As far as she's aware, I know a name on a crumpled piece of paper and nothing more.

'So, should we get that drink?' I ask quietly, attempting to carry on as we were before. 'Mum?'

Her face pales to a deathly-white as she struggles to form a sentence.

'Sa... Sadie...' She begins, her voice thick with emotion. 'I'm... I'm not feeling too well. I... I'm going to head home...'

'Okay.' Trying to not be fazed by her reaction, I reach for my handbag. 'Let me get my keys. I'll drive you back...'

'No!' She interrupts, shaking her head dramatically. 'I'll walk. I think... I think I need some fresh air.'

Without waiting for a response, she turns on her heel and marches out of the house. The sound of the front door slamming shut echoes throughout the empty cottage, causing my ears to ring with shock. The kitchen feels eerily quiet as I stare fixedly at the clock on the wall. With each second that passes my heart sinks lower and lower in my chest, until all that is left is a hollow shell where it once was.

They say it's better to have loved and lost than to have never loved at all, and where my dad is concerned, it seems I will never know...

Chapter 10

Trudging through the field of trees, I fill my lungs with fresh country air and focus on putting one foot in front of the other. The evening sun is now low in the sky, casting a warm glow across the dense woodland up ahead. Breathing deeply, I listen to the sound of broken branches snapping beneath my trainers as I follow the trodden footpath through the forest.

'Thank you for coming.' I mumble, not daring to look up in case I burst into tears. 'You didn't have to.'

'It's no problem.' Aidan replies easily, offering me a kind smile. 'Whenever you need a friend, you just have to say the word and I'll be there.'

Nodding gratefully, I concentrate on walking as we approach the famous rock at the edge of the woods. Still reeling from my earlier altercation with my mum and I guess... *my dad*, I picked up the phone and dialled Aidan's number. I don't know why. Aldo is usually my first port of call in a crisis, but today, Aidan was the person who came to mind. His face was the only one I wanted to see and his shoulder the only one I wanted to cry on.

Within thirty minutes of making the call, Aidan and I found ourselves here, at The Edge, and we have been trawling through the forest ever since. With it being early evening, the area is entirely deserted, which suits me perfectly. Coming to a stop at the verge of the cliff, I look down at the impressive view below and manage to raise a tiny smile.

'Wow.' Aidan remarks, taking a step closer to the edge.

'I know.' Dropping my bag by my feet, I take a seat on the rock and wrap my arms around my knees. 'No matter how many times I come here, it always makes me feel better. It never loses its magic, regardless of how terrible I feel.'

Joining me on the stone, Aidan mimics my movements and swings his legs over the edge.

'So, how are you getting on with the barn?' I ask, keeping my stare fixed on a tiny plane in the distance. 'Do you have any idea of a completion date yet?'

'Nice try.' Aidan replies quickly, a tone to his voice I don't recognise.

'I'm sorry?'

'I'm not discussing *me* until you tell me about *you.*' He says authoritatively, giving me a knowing look. 'Feel free to take your time. We can sit here all night if we must, but I'm not letting you go until you tell me what's upset you.'

Hanging my head, I let out a groan that makes my bones physically ache and close my eyes.

'It's such a long story.' I whisper, not knowing where to begin with the absurd few days I have had. 'A *really* long story.'

'Well, it's a good job I've got a lot of time...'

Smiling up at Aidan, I take a deep breath and start right at the very beginning. Taking myself back to the time I first asked about my biological father causes my heart to plummet to the floor. I recall the day I jumped into the car, piece of paper in hand, feeling more desperate than I ever had before. I tell him about the now infamous first meeting and the downward spiral it sent me into. I tell him about the familiar-looking builder I discovered working on the cottage. I relive the awful moment I realised who he really was...

Tears prick at the corners of my eyes as I finish with the unbelievable scene that unfolded in my kitchen just a couple of hours ago, and the devastation I felt when both Gavin and my mum left me there alone.

Waiting for him to respond, I pick up a branch and focus on breaking it into tiny pieces.

'I don't really know what to say.' He whispers, after a rather long silence. 'I'm so sorry, Sadie.'

'You don't need to be sorry.' I reply, desperately trying to control my wavering bottom lip. 'It's not your fault I'm in this mess.'

'And it wasn't *your* fault I was in mine, but you made it your mission to help me anyway.' Aidan says calmly. 'From what you have just told me, this situation with your father isn't *anyone's* fault, but that doesn't stop it from being a terribly sad situation. There's probably a lot of wrong turns been made on both sides, but unless you speak to both of them, they won't be able to make things right. You deserve to know your father and they deserve a chance to make that happen for you.'

Despite my efforts to stop the tears from falling, I erupt into a series of inconsolable sobs.

'There isn't a man in the world who wouldn't be proud to have a daughter like you, Sadie.' He continues, sliding over to me and wrapping an arm around my shoulder. 'It might seem impossible right now, but this story *could* have a happy ending...'

No longer trying to fight it, I allow myself to cry into Aidan's chest. The sadness in my heart becomes heavier with each tear that falls, but once I start, I just can't stop. I'm crying for my eight-year-old self, who would wonder why she didn't have a dad like the dads she saw at the school gates. I'm crying for fifteen-year-old Sadie, who would look at the cards on Father's Day mournfully, and I'm crying for the heartbroken woman, who just had her estranged dad run out on her.

Seconds, minutes, or even hours could have drifted by as we sit together at the top of the cliff, but when I finally tear myself away from Aidan's arms the land ahead is cast in complete darkness.

'You don't need to be strong all the time, Sadie.' Aidan says reassuringly, reaching over and wiping a stray tear from my cheek. 'It's okay not to be okay...'

Just when I was starting to feel a little better, my blood runs cold at his words. *It's okay not to be okay.* Aidan continues to talk, but I'm no longer listening to what he is saying. The last time I heard those six little words was on the worst day of my life. Without prior warning, I am mentally transported back to that day. The day where Aldo discovered me on my mum's bathroom floor after I had attempted to end my misery once and for all.

'Sadie?' Aidan presses, tilting my chin up to face him. 'Did you hear what I said?'

Shaking my head, I try and fail to fake a smile.

'I hate seeing you like this. I wish there was something I could do to make you feel better.' He groans, his brow creasing into a frown. 'How about I take you out? Let me take you for dinner tonight and you can forget about all of this for a little while.'

My heart wants to say yes, but my head just doesn't feel up to it.

'I don't know...'

'I'm not saying I can make your problems disappear, but I can make them go away for a little while and give you a chance to make sense of all this.'

Touched by his kind offer, I shake my head sadly.

'Thank you, Aidan, but I'm really not in the mood to go out tonight. I think I'm just going to go home and have an early night. Hopefully, things won't seem as bad in the morning.'

'Tomorrow then.' He persists, obviously in no hurry to give up. 'Look at it as a thank you for everything you have done for me.'

Resting my chin on my knees, I look up at him and feel my heart lift.

'Come on, Sadie. It's just one dinner. It's the least I can do.'

For the first time that evening, I smile and genuinely mean it.

'Tomorrow then.' I whisper, not taking my eyes off his. 'Tomorrow it is...'

Chapter 11

Standing by the window, I look out at the leafy lane and rest my hands on my hips. It's just before nine and there's still no sign of Jason and his team. They have formed a habit of arriving annoyingly early, resulting in me having to dive out of bed with just moments to spare, but today, I am ready and waiting for them. Gavin Gastrell knows who I am and there's no getting away from it. I can't rewind the clock and I can't pretend it didn't happen, because it did, and now I am going to have to tackle it head-on.

I tried to call my mum last night and again this morning, but unsurprisingly she didn't answer, nor did she try to call me back. I don't quite know what I was planning on saying to her, but I can't leave things the way they are. A part of me was relieved when she didn't pick up, because I was too scared to hear what she had to say. Would she use this as the catalyst to finally address the subject of my father, or would she refuse to acknowledge it and move on? Knowing my mum, it would probably be the latter.

Checking the time on my phone once more, I frown when I realise they are officially very late. In the two weeks they have been here, Jason hasn't arrived less than half an hour early. His absence this morning is telling me something has most definitely gone awry.

Reluctantly tearing myself away from the window, I open my laptop and pull up my emails in a bid to pass some time. After informing the support group about the upcoming fundraiser, it appears they haven't held back in sharing the news. I have been inundated with messages from people wanting to get involved. From members of the public offering their time, to local businesses wishing to donate items to the tombola. In just a few days, we have sold hundreds of tickets. That's *hundreds* of people ready and waiting to show up and donate to such a worthy cause.

I should be overjoyed. I should be delighted that I have received such a positive response already, but all I can think about is Gavin Gastrell and why the hell he isn't here. Well, I think I could take a good guess as to why he isn't here. He most likely isn't here because he has to face the reality that he has *three* children and not two. He most likely isn't here because he has just seen the woman he ran out on two decades ago and he most likely isn't here because...

Hearing a commotion outside, I push myself up and head over to the window. They're here! *Finally!* Running down the hallway, I quickly throw open the door and wave my arms in the air.

'Jason!' I yell, causing him to look up as he trudges down the garden path with a pair of ladders over his shoulder.

'Morning, Sadie.' Placing the ladders on the doorstep, Jason gives me a concerned look. 'Are you alright, love?'

'I'm fine.' I lie, desperately looking behind him for Gavin. 'You're just a bit late, that's all.'

Pulling a phone out of his pocket, Jason frowns at the screen and nods.

'Yeah, I'm sorry about that. One of the lads called in sick, so I had a bit of a mad half an hour calling around to find a temp.'

'Oh...' I reply, trying to hide how agitated I am. 'Which... which one was it?'

'Gav.' Rolling his eyes, Jason scratches a blob of dried paint off his arm. 'Funny thing is, Gav's normally the responsible one. Just shows, doesn't it? You can't rely on bloody anyone these days.'

'I couldn't agree more...' I mumble, feeling completely deflated.

'Can I take these through, love?' Jason asks, tapping his ladders. 'The other lads will be here shortly.'

'Yes, of course.' I stammer. 'Will Gavin be back tomorrow?'

'You've got to be joking!' Jason chuckles. '*None* of us will be here tomorrow, love. You don't pay us enough to work weekends. Don't worry though, we'll be back on Monday. That goes for Gav, too.'

Smiling back at him, I allow the door to close and lean against the wall in frustration. I spent all morning and most of last night planning each and every word I would say to him, but he's not here. Now, the words I spent so long organising in my mind are just rolling around in there aimlessly. Tangling themselves up in the warped feelings I have desperately been trying to make sense of.

Hearing the usual drilling noises drift out of the kitchen, I slowly make my way up the stairs. With the elusive Gavin Gastrell not coming back until Monday, if at all, and my mum refusing to answer my messages, I don't quite know what to do with myself. The only two people in the world who can help me to figure this out are avoiding me like the plague. What was once a taboo subject for my mother and I has jumped out of the shadows and hit us both straight in the face. I can understand how difficult this must be for both of them, but they are going to have to address this sooner or later.

A tiny *meow* drifts out of my bedroom as I come to a stop on the landing, inviting me in for a much-needed snuggle. Curling up on the bed next to a purring Mateo, I try to rationalise the awful signs of anxiety that are slowly coming back to haunt me. The unmoveable sense of dread, the constant feeling of fear that is impossible to shake off, and the sadness of simply not knowing what tomorrow will bring.

Not wanting to allow the angst and worry to take over me, I push them to the back of my mind and grab my mirror from the bedside table. Without meaning to, I immediately start comparing myself to Gavin. Our eyes are identical. Not slightly similar, they're *exactly* the same. I've always wondered where my emerald eyes came from, because my mother certainly doesn't have them, but now I know. The same freckles that are scattered across my nose are evident on his and our matching button noses are there for all to see.

Why has it taken me so long to see what is now so blindingly obvious? That dreaded day when I drove to his address, I didn't see a thing. I couldn't find anything at all in his face that connected us, but now the similarities are impossible to ignore.

As I stare into the mirror, my face slowly morphs into his, causing a wave of nausea to wash over me. I've always believed that you shouldn't open a can of worms unless you're completely confident you can handle the consequences, but until that can is open, how can you *possibly* be certain?

Chapter 12

After two hours of contouring, highlighting and preening my face to perfection, the girl in the mirror no longer resembles Gavin Gastrell in the slightest. Her lips are ruby red and her eyes are lined in a black darker than the sky at midnight. All traces of the man I am trying so desperately hard not to think about have vanished and I couldn't be more relieved about it.

Applying a final sweep of blusher to the apples of my cheeks, I close my cosmetic case and smile happily at my reflection. Aidan is due to collect me for our dinner in fifteen minutes and despite my disappointment over Gavin's absence this morning, I have actually enjoyed getting ready. I didn't anticipate putting this much effort into my appearance, but one thing led to another and I've somehow found myself with bouncy curls and a heavily made-up face. My favourite little black dress and Suave stilettos complete my glamorous look perfectly, giving my confidence a welcome boost.

Some might say I look a little overdone for a simple thank-you dinner with a... *friend*, but with each layer of slap I piled on and each spritz of perfume I applied, the sadness inside me slowly ebbed away. Beautifying myself has been a distraction that I desperately needed.

Taking my phone from my clutch bag, I frown when I realise my mum still hasn't responded to my attempts to contact her. Eight unanswered phone calls, four ignored text messages and a couple of unreturned emails. Bringing up my messages folder once more, I start to type out yet another text message and stop when I realise I don't know what else I can say. If eight missed calls aren't enough to make her want to contact me, I don't think another *Can you give me a call, please?* text is going to have much effect.

Deciding to call Aldo instead, I select his number from my contact list and hold the handset to my ear. Since our spontaneous wine night a few days back, I haven't seen or heard from him. His usual moody voicemail drifts down the line and I tap my phone against my hand in confusion. It would appear my mum isn't the only one who's avoiding me at the moment. Before I can hit redial, bright lights outside the cottage catch my attention and I drop the handset back into my bag.

Peering through the glass, I smile to myself when I notice a black cab waiting by the side of the road. He's early. Ten minutes early, to be precise. Quickly making my way along the hallway, I smooth down my dress before reaching for the handle and pulling open the door.

The silhouette that stands before me is hidden by the darkness of night, but I know it certainly doesn't belong to Aidan. It's too tall, it's too broad and it's far too imposing. Flicking on the light, I feel my blood run cold as the person on my doorstep is revealed. The leather jacket, the perfect stubble, the trademark streak of grey in his dark hair...

Stepping into view, Spencer Carter flashes me a smile that makes my stomach drop to the floor. His chiselled face is illuminated by the light behind me, making him look like a mirage as he takes another step towards me.

'Sadie...' He says softly, his dark eyes glistening. 'You look amazing.'

His familiar aftershave hits me like a punch to the gut as he holds out his arms and envelopes me in a hug. His arms wrap around my narrow shoulders, causing my body to ache at the memory of him and the time we spent together.

'How... how did you find me?' I stammer, wriggling out of his grip.

The same charm he's always had oozes out of him as he leans against the doorframe confidently.

'Piper gave me your address.'

The mere mention of Piper causes my blood pressure to rise.

'Why? Why are you here?'

'I just had to find you, Sadie.' He replies effortlessly, as though the answer was so very obvious. 'I've wanted to find you for so long now, but I told myself to stay away. I told myself that you deserved better and that I had to move on and let you go, but I can't. I can't do it.'

My ears ring with adrenaline as I stare back at him. This cannot be happening. Not now. Not today. Not in this lifetime.

'You will never know how sorry I am for the way I treated you. I was stupid. I was foolish. I was *scared*. My feelings for you scared me, Sadie. They scared me more than you can ever know...' His dark eyes shine passionately, making my legs tremble with emotion. 'Losing you was the worst mistake I have ever made and I kick myself every single day for it. I should never have let you walk out of my life. I should never have let you go. You're The One, Sadie.'

'No...' I whisper, too shocked to know if I'm speaking out loud.

Seemingly oblivious to what I just said, Spencer continues with his speech regardless.

'If I could turn back the clock and right my wrongs, I would do so in a heartbeat. I *need* you in my life, Sadie. We're meant to be together...'

As much as I hate to admit it, he's right. He's totally right. Spencer Carter and I *were* meant to be together, but that was in a different lifetime. Our relationship ended just twelve months ago, but those twelve months might as well be a million years. We had our chance and he ruined it. He ripped out my heart and tore it into tiny pieces. He hurt me like I've never been hurt before and now he has come back. After a year of no contact, he's decided to declare his undying love for me. It's like he knew I was finally over him and couldn't resist coming back to ruin me one more time.

'You know it and I know it.' He persists, taking my hand in his. 'Please, Sadie, you have to forgive me.'

My chest becomes increasingly tight as I stumble back into the cottage in an attempt to walk away from him, but Spencer's words follow me inside.

'We were great together, Sadie, and we could be again. I've thought about you every night since you left. Don't tell me you haven't thought about me, because I know you have...'

Turning to face him, I feel my heart pang with longing. I want to scream at him. I want to be furious with him for coming here and turning my life upside down, but nothing comes out. I can't bring myself to say a word. I just stare back at him, wanting to hate him with everything I have, but the truth is, I don't.

'I *love* you, Sadie, and I know deep down, you still love me, too...' Spencer's voice trails off as the sound of footsteps echoes along the hall.

Looking behind him, I try to compose myself as Aidan walks into the living room with a bouquet of roses in his hand.

'Sadie?' He says, looking at Spencer cautiously. 'Is everything okay?'

'Yes.' I stammer frantically. 'Everything's fine.'

Not seeming convinced, Aidan simply nods in response and places the roses on the dining table.

Tucking my handbag under my arm, I turn to Spencer and lower my voice to a whisper.

'You have to leave.' I say weakly, trying to avoid looking him in the eye.

'Please don't push me away.' Placing a hand on my arm, Spencer attempts to pull me towards him. 'We need to talk...'

'Just go, Spencer!' I hiss, my bottom lip wobbling. 'I can't do this right now.'

Hesitantly letting go of my arm, Spencer looks Aidan up and down before reluctantly nodding and heading for the door.

'I meant every word I said.' He says sadly, his eyes almost convincing me this is true. 'And I'll mean it tomorrow, the next day and every day after that.'

Keeping my eyes fixed on the ground, I don't look up until he slips out of the cottage and into the waiting taxi outside. The sound of Spencer's cab zooming into the distance causes my heart to ache as Aidan comes to a stop beside me.

'Are you sure you're okay?' He asks, looking at me with great concern. 'I understand if you want to cancel?'

Shaking my head, I look into the mirror and take a deep breath.

'I'm fine. Let's go...'

*   *   *

Il Migliore. Without even asking, Aidan has chosen my favourite restaurant. He graciously pulled out my seat and immediately ordered a bottle of Moet, but all I can see is Spencer. Spencer Carter with his stupid grey streak, battered leather jacket and annoyingly beautiful eyes. The image of him standing on my doorstep is etched into my mind, and nothing Aidan can do will take it away.

'You look lovely.' Aidan remarks, stopping my train of thought. 'You look really, incredibly beautiful.'

'Thank you.' Resting my elbows on the table, I look around the bustling restaurant. 'I just rolled out of bed like this...'

Laughing at my lame attempt at a joke, Aidan leans back in his seat as a waiter places two fresh glasses on our table. As usual, Il Migliore is as busy as it could possibly be. Everywhere you look couples are enjoying fine dining by candlelight. Champagne corks are popping and laughter is dancing in the air. It's such a beautiful setting for what should be a beautiful evening, but there's a big Spencer-shaped cloud hanging over it.

'That's a sad smile.' Aidan remarks, studying my face closely. 'I take it my efforts at making you feel better are failing miserably?'

His face falls and I suddenly feel guilty for allowing Spencer to ruin our evening after Aidan has gone to so much trouble.

'I'm sorry.' Plastering my best faux smile on my face, I reach for my glass and take a tiny sip. 'I'm just a little thrown, that's all.'

'I'm guessing this is in reference to a certain gentleman I discovered at the cottage when I arrived?' He says solemnly. 'Whoever he is, you didn't look too happy to see him.'

The truth is, I *was* happy to see him. Well, *happy* probably isn't the right word, but the moment my eyes met his, all those old feelings came flooding back to me and I was powerless to stop them.

'That was Spencer.' I admit, hating the way my skin tingles as his name crosses my lips. 'My ex-fiancé.'

Aidan's eyes widen as he waits for me to elaborate, but I'm not sure I want to continue.

'Go on...' He pushes gently.

'We... we broke up around a year ago.' Smiling at a passing waiter, I bring my fork to my lips before placing it back down on the plate. 'I haven't spoken to him since.'

'Him turning up like that must have been quite a shock for you.' Aidan replies.

'It was like being hit by a truck, to be perfectly honest. I opened the door expecting to see you and there he was. Just like the last twelve months hadn't happened...' Forcing myself to take a bite of my food, I chew and swallow before continuing. 'He was my everything. We were engaged to be married and deliriously happy, or so I thought. It turns out that I was the only one who was happy. Spencer was just being dragged along for the ride.'

'I see...' Aidan muses, an expressionless tone to his voice. 'I take it this relationship didn't end well?'

'You could say that.' Sadness hits me once more and I push away my plate. 'Spencer decided quite abruptly that things just weren't working out and I didn't take it very well. I was completely and utterly heartbroken. The breakup, coupled with other things, is what started my anxiety in the first place. The grief I felt from losing him just never left. If anything, it got bigger as the days passed by. To make matters worse, it wasn't long after our split that I discovered he had been seeing one of my best friends before we... before *he* called it a day.'

'Ouch...' Not giving anything away as he soaks up every word I'm saying, Aidan stares down at the table thoughtfully.

'He treated me badly, I can't deny that, but seeing him again took me right back to when we were together. I've been so busy these past few months that I've managed to block him out. I forced all thoughts of him into the little box at the back of my mind and pretended that it never really happened, but it did.'

Looking down at the tattoo on my ring finger, I smile sadly. 'The sight of him made my heart hurt like crazy. I want to hate him so badly, but I just can't. It probably sounds pathetic to you, but I genuinely believed he was The One.'

A group of women carrying birthday balloons gather around the table behind us and Aidan waits until they're seated before speaking.

'It doesn't sound pathetic at all. The first time I set eyes on Mel, I knew she was the woman I would marry.' He says fondly, running his thumb over the white band on his finger where a wedding ring once resided. 'I genuinely believed Mel was my future, but life doesn't always work out the way we plan.'

Hearing Mel's name is enough to make me realise what Spencer put me through was nothing in comparison to what some people have to deal with.

'So, what did he want?' Aidan asks, steering the conversation back to Spencer. 'What did he have to say for himself?'

'He said that he was sorry. He said he had made a terrible mistake and asked me to forgive him.' Knowing how ridiculous this sounds considering how he treated me, I feel my cheeks blush with embarrassment. 'He said losing me was the worst regret of his life and he wanted to start again.'

Aidan raises his eyebrows and pulls his glass towards him.

'How do you feel about that?'

I stare into the distance and consider his question carefully. How do I feel about it? *Sad, bewildered, dazed, annoyed, angry, frustrated.*

'In the three minutes I spent with him before you arrived, I probably felt every emotion imaginable, but the one that's still with me now is relief.' I admit honestly. 'Relief that our relationship wasn't something I imagined and relief that he's finally realised his mistake.'

'And where does that leave you?' Running his fingers through his hair, Aidan stares back at me blankly. 'Where do you go from here?'

'I really don't know. My head is telling me to shut the door and not look back, but I can't deny that a tiny part of my heart is screaming out for him.' Aidan's smile flickers and I hold my head in my hands. 'I know what you're thinking, but I can't help the way that I feel, can I? He's the only person in my entire life who has ever made me feel so loved, so wanted and so protected. I don't think anyone will ever make me feel that way again.'

There's an emotional silence between us, where the laughter from the table behind seems to be twice as loud as it was before.

'Do you remember what I said to you in the woods yesterday?' Aidan asks softly, leaning towards me as I shake my head in response. 'I told you that you were kind, generous, thoughtful, courageous and amazingly inspiring. You're selfless, caring, loving... the list is endless, and you're not even aware of it.' Resting his hand on my arm, Aidan smiles back at me. 'Sadie, you're one of the most beautiful people I've ever met, both inside and out.'

Feeling tears prick at the corner of my eyes, I furiously blink them back.

'You don't have to rely on just one person to love you. There are people out there who will love you more than he ever did. People who wouldn't ever hurt you the way he did in a million years.' Squeezing my arm gently, Aidan looks me straight in the eye. 'Please don't settle for someone who doesn't deserve you, because once you realise your true worth, walking away from those who don't value you will become the easiest thing you ever do...'

Chapter 13

Waiting for the traffic lights to change, I look at the road signs in front of me and consider my options. Left would take me to my mum's place and right would lead me straight to Aldo. With a bag of breakfast sandwiches on the passenger seat and Mateo in his carry case in the back, I hit the indicator and turn right. Considering the lack of contact from my mum, I don't think arriving unannounced would be a very good idea. Plus, after Spencer's appearance last night, I could really do with Aldo's advice.

Despite her disappearing act, I'm in no rush to see my mum. I feel as though I'm juggling so many plates at the moment and if I attempt to pick up another one, they're all going to come crashing down around me. First the fundraiser, then Gavin and now Spencer. Just last week, life seemed so very simple. Aidan had come back to Cheshire and things were looking rather rosy indeed. Little did I know then what was coming my way, but the world keeps on spinning and I carry on regardless.

The funny thing about juggling problems is, it's like carrying a pile of laundry. You bend down to pick up a single sock and the rest of the clothes fall to the ground. The more you try to pick up, the more you find yourself dropping. Whereas if you carry on walking to the washing machine, you might lose a few socks along the way, but the majority of the laundry will make it there. You just have to keep going. You just have to put one foot in front of the other, telling yourself that *this too shall pass*. It might pass like a kidney stone, but it *will* pass....

Pulling on the handbrake, I look out of the window at Aldo's house and frown. The drapes are closed and the collection of milk bottles on the doorstep indicates no one has been home for quite some time. Unbuckling my seatbelt, I walk up to the door and peer through the frosted glass. There's a pile of unopened letters on the mat, a stack of pizza boxes piled up on top of the bin and a dishevelled Aldo trundling down the stairs. Giving him a wave, I head back to the car for Mateo and the breakfast sandwiches.

'Heavy night?' I ask, raising my eyebrows as he opens the door.

Wearing last night's clothes and a scowl that could curdle milk, Aldo scratches his stubble and yawns.

'You could say that.' He replies groggily, grabbing one of the milk bottles.

'I thought as much!' I scold. 'That's why you didn't answer my calls, isn't it? You've been on another bloody bender. You're getting too old for all these crazy nights out now, Aldo. You're not twenty-one... '

'Edward moved out yesterday.'

Stopping in my tracks, I turn around and wait for him to say that he's joking.

'You're kidding?'

'I told him I believed our relationship had run its course and he agreed.' He says downheartedly. 'There was no point in dragging it out.'

Placing the brown paper bag on the kitchen island, I rest my hands on my hips as I listen to him speak.

'Within an hour of us having the conversation, Edward called a removal van and off he went. Just like that.' Aldo looks around the sparse kitchen and shakes his head. 'It was like he was never here...'

'And how do you feel now that he's gone?' I ask, already having a pretty good idea.

'This is what I wanted, so I have no choice but to be happy about it.' He grumbles, taking a bobble from his wrist and twisting his hair into a bun. 'I just didn't think it would happen so quickly, that's all.'

Freeing Mateo from his crate, I offer Aldo one of the sandwiches.

'I thought he would at least fight for me and for what we had.' He continues, tearing off the wrapper and taking a huge bite. 'He must have been just as unhappy as I was.'

I frown as I watch him devour his breakfast hungrily, all the while keeping his scowl firmly in place.

'I hate to say this, Aldo, but you don't seem very happy to see him go.' I admit honestly. 'What exactly did you say to him?'

'That's the funny thing, I only had to say *I think we should take a break* and he was reaching for his suitcase. He agreed that we were stuck in a rut and said our lives were heading in different directions. He couldn't get out of here quickly enough.'

'Have you spoken to him since?'

'No and I don't want to.' Wandering into the living room with Mateo at his heels, Aldo tosses the sandwich wrapper into the paper bin. 'I don't want to talk to him or to anyone else about this right now.'

Recognising from his tone of voice that it's time to drop the subject, I decide to try a different tact.

'It's a beautiful day.' I say encouragingly, opening the drapes and clearing away the empty bottles from the coffee table. 'What do you have planned for today?'

'Nothing.' Collapsing onto the couch, Aldo reaches for the remote and flicks on the television.

'Well, you can't sit around here all morning. It's glorious outside! I'm going to the village later to collect donations for the fundraiser tomorrow, why don't you join me?'

'I don't know...'

'Oh, come on.' I persist, trying my hardest to make this sound like the most exciting activity ever. 'It will be fun.'

'Our ideas of *fun* are obviously miles apart, but if it will shut you up, I'll do it.'

Grinning happily, I silently cheer at my success in coaxing him out of the house.

'On one condition.' He adds, stroking Mateo as he curls up on his lap.

'And what's that?'

'That I get to keep this fleabag for tonight.'

I glance at Mateo, who is nuzzling into Aldo's chest like a tiny baby, and bite my lip. Aldo's pretend hatred of Mateo is something we always joke about, but keeping him overnight is extremely out of character.

'What do you say, Mateo? Do you want to stay with Uncle Aldo?'

'*Meow!*'

'I'll take that as a yes...'

*　*　*

Accepting an enormous hamper from the friendly shop assistant, I tick the quirky boutique off my list and shake her hand firmly.

'Thank you so much.' I say gratefully, balancing the wicker basket on my shoulder. 'You have been incredibly generous. I'll be sure to put your details on the flyers.'

Struggling to carry the heavy hamper, I pause by the novelty napkins and look around the shop in search of Aldo. Quickly discovering him with his nose in a scented candle, I motion for him to help me with the parcel.

'Seven down, three to go.' I sigh, passing him the selection of luxury toiletries. 'People are so generous when it comes to charity. It really restores your faith in mankind, doesn't it?'

Mumbling something I don't quite catch in response, Aldo takes my keys out of his pocket and beeps open the boot of the car.

'Don't you feel so much better for getting out into the sunshine?' Watching him place the hamper amongst the rest of the donated goods, I stand under the shop's canopy to escape the sweltering sun. 'It seems you're not a vampire after all.'

'Where to next?' He replies, ignoring my question completely.

Looking up and down the busy lane, I point to a restaurant across the street.

'I believe Viaan have offered a voucher. Champagne dinner for two with all the trimmings.'

'Champagne dinner? I don't suppose you can fix it for me to win that?' Aldo jokes, a slight twinkle playing on the corner of his mouth.

'There will be no fixing of any of the prizes.' I chastise, hitting his arm playfully. 'If you want the dinner, you're going to have to buy a ticket. You have to be in it to win it.'

Linking my arm through his as we head inside the restaurant, I catch the manager's eye and lead Aldo over to the bar area.

'I'll be with you in two minutes, Sadie!' Jay shouts, as he shows a couple of businessmen to their seats. 'Get yourselves a drink on the house.'

Before I can look through the menu, one of the bartenders whips up two cold cocktail glasses and places them on the counter in front of us.

'Don't mind if I do.' Aldo says happily, giving the barman the thumbs-up sign and hopping onto a stool. 'I'll have yours, Shirley. You're driving.'

I roll my eyes and slide my glass over to Aldo. I should have known the quickest way to cheer him up was to take him to a bar.

'There you go.' I grumble. 'Enjoy.'

Leaving him to devour his drinks, I lean against the bar and look around the popular eatery. Contagious laughter floats into the restaurant from the busy gardens outside and I strain my neck to have a quick peek. Despite it only being midday, people are making the most of their weekends by supping ice-cold drinks in the sunshine. Children are running between the tables with balloons tied to their wrists and families are enjoying each other's company over Viaan's signature dishes. It really is as pretty as a picture.

Just as I am tearing my eyes away, a flash of black catches my attention and I feel my heart skip a beat. Moving closer, I quickly recoil when my suspicions are confirmed. Spencer Carter, as I live and breathe. Feeling frozen to the spot, I watch him laugh and joke with a man I don't recognise and try not to panic. I told him to go. I told him to leave!

'Should we take these into the gardens?' Aldo asks, sliding off his seat. 'It sounds like that's where the party's at.'

'No!' I yell, reaching out and grabbing his sleeve. 'I... erm... actually, can you go over to Golden Glow and ask Louisa for the gift box she offered?'

Holding up his glass, Aldo reaches for a straw from behind the bar.

'Let me finish my drinks and then I'll go...'

'Please can you go now?' Spencer's iconic laugh echoes into the room, causing my heart to race with alarm. 'She closes early today and I really don't want to miss her.'

Swearing under his breath, Aldo reluctantly abandons his drinks and makes his way out of the restaurant. A bead of sweat rolls down my temple as I watch him cross the street and push open the door to Golden Glow.

Breathing a sigh of relief that I seem to have dodged a bullet, I force a smile when Jay comes to a stop in front of me and holds out a gold envelope.

'Here you are. As promised.'

'Thank you, Jay.' Accepting the voucher, I reach up and give him a quick hug. 'You're a superstar.'

'It's my pleasure.' Jay replies, stifling a tired yawn. 'I'm terribly sorry to have kept you waiting. We've been incredibly busy today.'

'I can see that.' I say hurriedly, very aware that Spencer is just a few feet away. 'Well, don't worry, I won't keep you. Thanks again, Jay.'

Desperate to make my escape, I wave goodbye to the bartender and reach for the door handle. I can't let Aldo bump into Spencer before I've had the chance to tell him about what happened last night...

'Sadie!' Jay shouts, just as the door is closing behind me. 'I forgot to give you something...'

Turning around, I fix a smile on my face once more.

'Sorry, I completely forgot. We also wanted to donate this.' Handing me a bottle of vintage wine in a stunning presentation box, Jay pats my back and rushes off to a waiting customer.

'Thank you so much!' I shout after him. 'You're too kind.'

Clutching the expensive bottle to my chest, I reach for the handle once more and stop when I sense someone standing behind me.

'Thirsty?' A deep voice asks, causing the hairs on the back of my neck to stand on end.

Not daring to look up, I flinch as Spencer reaches out and tilts my chin up to face him.

'I've been trying to call you all day, but the line wouldn't connect.' He says in confusion, placing his bottle of beer on the bar behind us. 'You didn't block my number, did you?'

'Something like that.' I reply, trying to keep my voice steady and failing miserably.

'I also stopped by your cottage again this morning, but you weren't home.' Tilting his head to one side, he reads the writing on the front of the envelope from Jay. 'A charity fundraiser? How very twee...'

'What do you want from me, Spencer?' I snap in annoyance, frustrated by his laidback attitude.

A flicker of hurt hits his eyes and I immediately feel bad.

'Well?' I persist, suddenly feeling rather powerful as I watch him struggle to get his words out.

'I want you.' He says eventually, looking over his shoulder to ensure no one else can hear our conversation. 'Just you, Sadie. That's all I want. Nothing more and nothing less.'

'How dare you?' I whisper, my voice trembling with a fury I didn't know I had. 'How dare you come back to me after all this time? After the way you treated me? After Ivy? And after everything else you put me through?'

Leading me into a quiet corner of the restaurant, Spencer grins at a passing customer and holds me at arm's length.

'You're angry, Sadie, I get that, but you have to believe me when I say that I made a terrible mistake. I'm only human. I'm allowed to make a mistake, aren't I?'

I stare into the eyes I once loved and shake my head incredulously.

'A mistake is forgetting to pay a bill or leaving a red sock in the laundry. Breaking someone's heart, treating them like dirt and sleeping with one of their closest friends is *not* a mistake. It's cruel, heartless and unforgiveable.'

Spencer's eyes glass over and he looks down at the ground dejectedly.

'If you want me to stop trying, Sadie, just say the words and I'll stop. I'll walk away and I promise you won't hear from me ever again.'

'Trying?' I scoff. 'You call ambushing me at my home and in a busy restaurant *trying?*'

Responding with a simple nod of the head, he quickly finishes his beer and slips a crisp note under the bottle.

'Point taken.' He says confidently, digging his phone out of his pocket and heading for the door. 'But it's always been you, Sadie. It always has been and it always will be.'

Watching him leave, I try to steady my breathing as all the blood drains from my face. Half with relief and half with sadness that he's left. Inwardly kicking myself for allowing him to get to me again, I spring into action as an extremely shocked and appalled Aldo walks into Viaan.

'What the f...'

'Don't.' I hiss, ushering him outside before he can cause a scene. 'Just get in the car.'

Looking understandably floored, Aldo's jaw drops open as I hastily push him into the passenger seat.

'What was that all about?' He demands, looking over his shoulder as though he's expecting to see Spencer chasing us down the lane. 'Did you know he was up here?'

Turning the engine over, I indicate before pulling out onto the road and bite my lip guiltily.

'Yes...'

'*Yes?*' Aldo repeats loudly, twisting his body to face me. 'Shirley, what the hell is going on?'

Waiting until we hit a quiet part of the lane, I turn into a lay-by and bring the car to a steady stop.

'Spencer came to Blossom View last night.' I explain, watching the stream of cars whizz past along the road. 'He told me that he'd made a huge mistake and you can guess the rest.'

'You told him to take a running jump, right?' Aldo whispers in horror. 'Please tell me that you did, because I don't have the energy right now to deal with...'

'Of course, I did!' I interrupt, shooting him a frustrated scowl.

'Then why am I only just hearing about this?' Annoyance is plastered across Aldo's face as he glares back at me angrily. 'If you told him to crawl back under his rock and leave you alone, why didn't you tell me about this earlier?'

'I intended to!' I exclaim. 'That's why I arrived with breakfast this morning, but when you told me about Edward I decided to keep it to myself. You've got enough on your own plate.'

'Remember what happened the last time you tried to keep your problems to yourself?' He says accusingly. 'Spencer is the main reason you went through what you did. I won't stand by and allow him to do it again.'

'Just because I couldn't cope then, doesn't mean I can't cope now.' I reply, rather haughtily. 'You have no idea of how much I have dealt with on my own lately. No idea at all...'

'What's that supposed to mean?' He retorts, narrowing his eyes at me suspiciously.

'Like Spencer coming back. Like discovering one of the builders working on my house is actually my dad. Like carrying the worry about why my mum has ignored me ever since. Like...'

'Stop right there!' Aldo interjects sharply. 'What the hell are you talking about now?'

Holding my head in my hands, I chastise myself for not being able to keep my mouth shut. Realising that I now have to fill Aldo in on the events of late, I take a couple of deep breaths before reliving the past week of my life.

'So, there you have it.' I say sadly, finally finishing my story and starting the ignition. 'But as I said before, I'm fine with it. All of it.'

Blinking repeatedly, Aldo tries to process the mammoth amount of information I've just told him.

'Shirley, hiding problems and dealing with them are *not* the same thing.' He says quietly, his voice suddenly solemn. 'Your dad turning up like this is bound to have an effect on you. You can't hide it and pretend it didn't happen, because we all know how that story ends.'

'I didn't hide it.' I object mildly, knowing that if I overreact he will take it as a sign of a meltdown. 'I just decided to deal with it by myself and I would appreciate it if you could respect that.'

After staring at me for a moment longer than necessary, Aldo grudgingly nods.

'Okay. Fine. So, tell me, how exactly do you intend on dealing with this?'

'To be honest with you, Aldo, I don't know yet.' Considering his question, I tap my fingers on the handbrake thoughtfully. 'I'm just going to take it one day at a time and cross each bridge as I come to it.'

Not seeming convinced in the slightest, Aldo looks straight ahead as we approach his house.

'Can I give you one piece of advice, Shirley?'

'Sure.' I reply breezily, knowing that I probably won't like what I'm about to hear.

'Before you cross those bridges you talk about, you might want to consider burning one or two and *never* looking back...'

Chapter 14

Turning onto my driveway, I unbuckle my seatbelt and rub my tired eyes. If my run-in with Spencer wasn't draining enough, hosting the Anxiety Anonymous meeting claimed any ounce of energy I had left. My muscles are physically aching with exhaustion and my head is throbbing due to the amount of overthinking I've been doing lately. All I want to do now is run myself a bubble bath and relax until the fundraiser tomorrow. With Mateo keeping Aldo company for the night, I should have no excuse to not have an early night and recharge my batteries.

Swinging my keys around my finger, I walk down the garden path and frown when I spot a tall parcel on my doorstep. The sleek black box is wrapped in a delicate gold ribbon, without a hint as to where it has come from. Struggling to lift it, I unlock the door and drag the intriguing box in behind me. Not bothering to take my jacket off, I drop down onto the bottom step of the stairs and use my car keys to break the seal.

Lilies. Dozens of lilies. Carefully stroking the soft petals, I immediately sneeze and reach into my pocket for a tissue. I've always hated lilies. They remind me of funerals, doctors clinics and not to mention they set my allergies off. You would think Spencer would know that, wouldn't you? I don't even need to look at the card to know these are from him. Every single time he did something wrong he would present me with lilies and every single time I would thank him for the gesture and politely remind him how much I hate them. It seems a leopard really doesn't change its spots.

Closing the lid, I step over the glossy box and notice a tiny white envelope on the mat behind the door. Bending down to retrieve it, I smooth out the crumpled envelope in my hand. The paper is creased beyond recognition and a previous name has been crossed out in favour of mine. Ignoring the blatant attempt at recycling, I open the envelope and pull out a torn piece of paper.

> *Sadie,*
> *I found this and thought of you.*
> *You know where I am if you need a friend.*
> *Aidan.*

Shaking the envelope, I place the piece of paper on the stairs as a daisy falls into the palm of my hand. Only, it's not just any old daisy. It's the most perfect daisy I have ever seen. Each and every petal is perfectly formed and the yellow stamen is brighter than the sun. It's flawless. Reading his note again, I carry the delicate flower into the living room and take a seat at the dining table.

> *I found this and thought of you.*

I pick up my phone to call him and pause when a thought suddenly hits me. Why did it make Aidan think of me? This daisy is perfect in every way. I'm not even close to being perfect. Quite the opposite, in fact. With Spencer seemingly intent on pushing his way back into my life and the situation with Gavin weighing heavily on my shoulders, I am half-expecting myself to crumble at any moment.

Aldo's right. Spencer leaving me *is* what started my anxiety all those months ago. And after how I've been feeling these past couple of days, there's no denying that Spencer Carter is most definitely a trigger for me. Only this time, the anxiety doesn't feel like a big black hole that I've fallen down and have no way to climb out of. It feels like a tiny blemish on a beautiful canvas. The rest of the picture is exactly as it should be, but I'm very aware of that one single mark. It's always there, at the back of my mind, but if I don't go looking for it, I barely notice it.

Maybe I am a stronger person now than I was back then. Maybe I have learnt from my past experience with anxiety. Maybe I am now fully equipped to deal with absolutely anything life throws at me.

As I say these statements to myself, I realise that I don't really believe them. Who am I trying to convince? Aldo? Aidan? The rest of the world? The truth is, the reason I keep telling myself these things is that I *have* to believe them. I don't have any other choice but to believe them, because there's no way I am returning to that dark place. Never again will I allow anxiety to chew me up and spit me out like it did the last time our paths crossed.

The dread, the darkness and the hollowness that consumed me have become my worst fears. Before my experience with anxiety I was scared of spiders, death and heights, but now none of that bothers me half as much as they used to. Instead, my greatest fear is fear itself and the most frightening thing about that is, fear is inside me at all times. It's down to me to keep it at bay. No one else can do it for me. No one else can stop it from happening again.

Before I can shake it off, an awful feeling creeps over me like a black cloak, casting a shadow of doubt over how far I have come. Knowing that if I allow it to sink its teeth into me I will slowly crumble to its powers, I push myself up and head into the kitchen.

Opening a window for some air, I lean against the sink and take a few deep breaths as my heart starts to race. My gaze lands on the sparkling granite counters and my heart beats even faster. Gavin Gastrell is all around me. He's here, even when he's not. I'm never going to be free of him. My ears start to ring and my chest becomes unbearably tight, despite my attempts to keep calm.

I slide down onto the cold tiles as my palms sweat like crazy. Resting my head between my legs, I desperately try to block out the rest of the world and focus on slowly counting to ten over and over again until the feeling finally subsides. Not daring to look up until I'm confident my heart rate has returned to normal, I lift my head and cautiously look around the kitchen. It's gone. The surge of adrenaline that was whooshing through my veins has finally stopped, but the sense of worry is still very much with me. The fear has crept into my stomach and is refusing to leave. It's toying with me. It's enjoying teasing me with a taste of what it is capable of.

That sinking feeling has dug its claws into me, but I refuse to let it bite. It's had its fun, it's tested my limits and it's discovered that I'm still susceptible to its wicked ways, but it stops right here. Anxiety can test me and torment me all it wants, but I don't want to play. I refuse to engage in its twisted games, because I won't be pushed back. I won't be afraid to continue living my life and I won't be its victim. Because I'm *not* a victim of anxiety. I *have* learnt from the past. My journey with anxiety has taught me more than I might dare to believe.

With a fresh surge of confidence, I reach into my pocket and hold the daisy to my chest. I'm Sadie Valentine and I will not be made to feel afraid by anxiety or any of the awful things it chooses to inflict on me. I will stand tall and feel safe in the knowledge that the power to beat anxiety lies within me, because I am Sadie Valentine and I *will* win...

Chapter 15

Tearing off a raffle ticket, I hand it to an excited child and slip the pad back into my apron pocket. His little face lights up as he waves the pink ticket in the air happily. Wishing him good luck in the tombola, I reorganise the cupcakes on the cake stand and admire the perfectly piped icing. The Anxiety Anonymous logo is emblazed everywhere for the world to see. It's printed on the balloons, it's splashed across the bunting and it's stamped on the t-shirts of all the support group members. If the primary aim of this fundraiser is to raise awareness of the charity, we can certainly tick that box.

Considering this event has been thrown together in such a short space of time, it's shaping up to be a huge success. The fundraiser has been in full swing for the past hour and despite a night of tossing and turning, I am playing the part of helpful assistant perfectly. With the help of an expertly rehearsed smile, I've managed to make it through the first sixty minutes without anyone knowing I am secretly panicking. There are hundreds of people milling around the stalls and attractions, but not one of them has a clue the smile I am flashing them is meaningless. The girl who shakes her donation bucket, coos at the animated children and merrily rips your stub in two when you cross the gate isn't really who you think she is. I might be making all the right noises, but inside, I am desperately trying to keep my anxiety at bay.

After my panic attack at Blossom View last night, I tried to take the positives from it and continue with the preparations for the fundraiser as though nothing had happened. Compared to the panic attacks I have experienced in the past, I managed to get it under control quickly and return to my evening without allowing it to scare me into submission. Not acknowledging its existence is one of my secret weapons in dealing with my anxiety and that's not to say I don't address that it's there. The anxiety is always with me, I just refuse to let it define the rest of my day. It can sit there, in the back of my mind, making my tummy feel queasy and my heart heavy with dread, but I won't back down. I will keep going for my own sanity and for all the people who have turned out to show their support today.

It's so ironic that shouting about anxiety from the rooftops is how we choose to raise awareness of the often taboo subject of mental health. The name of the charity itself declares anonymity, discretion and secrecy, but anxiety *shouldn't* be anonymous. Matters of the mind shouldn't ever be confined to a group of people who are only willing to seek help from behind the shield of remaining anonymous. The funny thing is, *no one* at my support group is anonymous. Far from it. Once they settle into the swing of things, each and every person I deal with is more than happy to share personal aspects of their life with other members of the group. The people I meet there aren't in attendance because they only feel comfortable under the cloak of anonymity. They're there because they want to talk about their anxiety with people who understand exactly what it is they are going through...

A new group of revellers arrive at the gate beside me and I fix a smile on my face as I accept their entry tickets and hand over charity wristbands. Pointing them in the direction of the bouncy castle, I make a scribble on my notepad and turn my attention to another waiting family.

'Sadie!' My mum's shrill voice shouts, above the sound of the music. 'Over here!'

'Hi, Mum!' I reply, between handing out wristbands. 'I'll be with you in just a minute.'

Quickly logging the entry tickets, I slip my hands into the pockets of my apron and turn to face her.

'How are you? I've been calling you for days.' I say casually, trying to appear nonchalant. 'Is everything okay?'

'I've not been too well.' She fires back, her false expression immediately giving away her lie. 'I intended to call you back, but you know how it is when your stomach isn't quite right.'

Not wanting to embarrass her, I choose to just go with it.

'I wasn't sure if you would come today.' Leaning against the table, I pass her a wristband and push my sunglasses into my hair. 'You ran out on me quite abruptly the other night.'

Her cheeks blush violently as she shoots me a frown.

'Like I said, my stomach hasn't been quite right.'

Recognising the look of panic on her face, I decide to breeze past it.

'What's with all the balloons?' I ask, pointing to the many animal-shaped balloons in her hand.

'They're Mick's. He's just parking the car.' She explains, jumping back to avoid a small child, who is impersonating a lion to mimic his painted face. 'Here, he made these this morning.'

'Thank you.' Gingerly accepting the balloons, I take a pin to one which is highly inappropriate and tie the rest to the entry gate. 'I'm guessing that one slipped the net?'

'Sorry about that. You know what he's like.' She stammers, tossing the popped balloon into the bin on her left. 'I don't suppose you have a moment to talk, do you?'

Already knowing where this conversation is heading, I focus on straightening the already-straight raffle books.

'What about?'

Biting her lip nervously, she shifts her weight from one foot to the other.

'Erm... well, I wanted to talk to you about... about...'

'Hi!' I exclaim, spotting Aldo making his way towards us with the Anxiety Anonymous logo drawn on his cheeks. 'Are you enjoying the festivities?'

'Trying to.' Glancing at my mum cautiously, Aldo gives her a polite nod. 'Linda.'

Grateful to have Aldo by my side, I return to the subject I least want to talk about.

'So, what did you want to talk to me about?'

Suddenly looking incredibly uneasy, she shakes her head as Mick strides across the car park behind us.

'It's not important.' She replies quickly, indicating that she's about to leave. 'I'll come and find you later.'

Smiling in response, I watch her walk away and silently curse myself. That was my chance. She was going to tell me about Gavin and I've just blown it. Removing my apron, I open my mouth to ask Aldo to watch the stall while I go after her when he beats me to it.

'There's something you need to know.' He starts, standing on the tips of his toes and looking around the busy field. 'It's Spencer. He's here.'

I feel my smile drop off my face as I turn to look in the direction he's pointing. Any courage I managed to gather up this morning leaves my body the second I spot him in the crowd of people. His infectious laughter spreads to those around him at an alarming rate. Like a virus, it takes hold of anyone who comes into contact with him. How? How does he do that? I used to think his ability to charm his way out of any situation was just one of his many amazing personality traits. Now it just feels fake, disingenuous and quite awful to witness. What I once admired as being charming is actually manipulation at its finest. Give him five minutes and Spencer Carter will convince you that grass is really pink, and not green as you have always believed. He'll convince you that he made a mistake. He will convince you that he is sorry and if you're not careful, he will convince you to take him back.

'Don't panic...' Aldo continues, brushing my hair out of my face. 'Just pretend that he isn't here. Keep calm and carry on.'

Keep calm and carry on. I repeat silently, wanting to laugh at how much easier said than done that is.

'Do you want me to get rid of him?' Aldo says suddenly, taking over and handing wristbands to a group of teenage girls. 'Just say the word and I'll chuck him out.'

Despite the growing panic inside me, I remain perfectly still and shake my head.

'No.' I reply eventually. 'Like you said, I'll just pretend he isn't here...'

'Yvette!' Aldo exclaims, discreetly nudging me in the ribs to alert me to her presence. 'What have you got there?'

Carrying a huge box on her shoulder, Yvette stops in front of us and hands over her entry ticket.

'It's organic soap.' Peeling open the lid to reveal many bars of soap bearing wonky Anxiety Anonymous logos, she grins proudly. 'I made them myself. I thought I could hand them out to people, if that's okay?'

'That's so kind of you.' I reply, as the music turns up a notch. 'Thanks, Yvette.'

Blushing at my praise, she moves the heavy box to her other shoulder.

'I'll get started!' She says excitedly. 'I don't want to miss your big speech. I've got Ruby calling on FaceTime to watch you!'

Giving her the thumbs-up, I'm quietly relieved when she takes her box and disappears into the sea of people. I want to run away. I want to race back to Blossom View and shut the door behind me. The idea of speaking in front of all these people is suddenly petrifying.

'You've got this, Shirley.' Aldo says confidently, rubbing my shoulders. 'Just think of it as one big support group, or do what I do and picture them all naked. Especially him over there by the doughnut stall.'

I know he's trying his best to be supportive, but he's just making me feel worse.

'Trust me.' Aldo continues. 'The naked thing works every time...'

The music comes to a sudden stop and I look up to see Julia striding across the stage with an Anxiety Anonymous banner draped across her blazer. Tapping the microphone, she beams brightly and waits for the crowd to fall into silence.

'Ladies and gentlemen, boys and girls...'

As Julia addresses her audience, I occupy myself with the cupcake stand and pretend to be engrossed in the intricate icing. No matter how big or small your anxiety is, trying to act like everything's okay is incredibly draining. The constant pretence eats away at your energy reserves, leaving just a fragile shell behind that will crumble at the slightest touch.

'Shirley, did you hear that?' Aldo squeals. 'After the next singer, it's your time to shine!'

'I just need to take five minutes.' I mumble, passing him my apron. 'Could you watch the gate for me?'

Not waiting for him to respond, I head for a clearing in the trees behind us. Leaving the noise of the fair behind, I walk into the woodland until the chaos fades into the distance. A couple of squirrels race past me as I come to a stop next to a fallen tree and take a seat on the trunk. *It's just a speech.* I tell myself. *A speech about a subject so close to your heart. A speech about a subject you have built an entire career around. You've got this, Sadie. You've got this.*

Filling my lungs with fresh air, I reach into my pocket and pull out the note from Aidan. The daisy is perfectly pressed between the two sides of paper, causing my spirits to instantly lift. Clutching it tightly, I take a few deep breaths and try to calm myself down. In just twenty minutes, the anxiety of having to speak publicly will have passed, but the root cause of my unease shall still be there and experience tells me it won't go anywhere until I address it.

Hearing the crowd burst into applause as the singer brings her set to an end, I retrace my steps and stumble out of the trees behind Aldo.

'There you are!' Aldo cries, visibly breathing a sigh of relief. 'I thought you had done a runner!'

Managing a tiny smile, I purse my lips as Julia takes to the microphone once more.

'Okay...' She says, in a gentle hypnotic voice that instantly captures everyone's attention. 'Now we have one of our very own counsellors, who has been on both sides of the anxiety fence, giving a short speech about her journey with mental health. Please welcome to the stage, Sadie Valentine.'

Another round of applause breaks out and a little push from Aldo encourages me to clumsily make my way to the platform. The ladder appears astronomically high as I reach for the railing and pull myself onto the stage. Heading over to the microphone, I politely shake Julia's hand as she gives me a reassuring smile and discreetly steps back into the shadows.

Looking out over the crowd, I see for the first time just how many people are here. Hundreds of pairs of eyes are fixed on me, all waiting to hear what I have to say. My mouth feels like sand and my palms start to sweat as I reach out and take the microphone. Tapping the top, I wince when an ear-piercing chime comes back at me.

'Hello...' I begin, holding up a hand and shyly waving at the crowd, causing them to laugh gently.

Taking Aldo's advice, I close my eyes for a second and imagine myself in the Anxiety Anonymous meeting room.

'I want to start by thanking you all for coming here today. It fills my heart with pride to see a community coming together like you have, but we all know that the real reason we are doing this is a lot more important than candyfloss and fairground rides...'

The slight chatter that was hanging in the air finally subsides, leaving the only noise coming from the speakers that are blasting my voice around the field.

'Anxiety Anonymous is a charity that offers support to thousands of anxiety sufferers up and down the country, but it's not enough. As many as one in four of us will be affected by mental health problems. It sounds quite scary that, doesn't it? I know when I was diagnosed with anxiety, that figure came as quite a shock to me. What had I ever done to be unlucky enough to be chosen? So many times, I asked myself, *why me?* What I really should have been asking was, why *not* me?'

Pausing for breath, I try to relax my vice-like grip on the microphone.

'To many people, anxiety is just a word. They simply aren't aware of the pain, the hurt and the devastation it can cause to the lives of those it ruins. And that's not because they're ignorant or because they choose to ignore it, but simply because we don't talk about it half as much as we should do.

Discovering Anxiety Anonymous is what gave me the confidence to speak about my own battle with anxiety. Without the help of the support group, I wouldn't be up here on this stage telling you my story. Anxiety Anonymous saved my life and for that, I will forever be grateful.'

A lady in the front row starts to clap and the rest of the crowd quickly join in.

'Anxiety shouldn't be a subject we are afraid to talk about and it most certainly shouldn't be anonymous. The word itself conjures up a sense of wrongfulness that you don't want to be connected with....'

Catching a glimpse of my mum in the crowd, my eyes widen in shock when I realise she is talking to Spencer. Laughing along, she swoons when he kisses her cheeks and compliments her new hairstyle. As I look on, Mick wraps an arm around Spencer's shoulder, as though he's the son he never had, and the two of them walk off in the direction of the bar. Their laughter echoes around the otherwise silent field, the only two in the crowd not being respectful and listening to what I have to say.

Feeling my confidence slowly ebb away, I move my gaze across the field and spot Aidan at the entry gate. Just the sight of him makes me feel instantly better as I am reminded of the pressed daisy in my pocket. Trying to get my speech back on track, I shake my head in an attempt to get my brain to focus.

Opening my mouth to speak once more, I look to the left and I'm shocked to discover Ivy, Piper and Zara filming me on their mobile phones. Their sniggers shout out to me, causing memories of what led me to the support group in the first place to spring into my mind like a film reel. My breakup with Spencer, the girls I thought were my friends, my strained relationship with my mum and Gavin Gastrell. Only, the last one isn't a flashback. Gavin Gastrell is actually here.

Standing at the far right of the crowd, Gavin, Paige, Mitch and Angela have been listening to me intently as I speak. Their committed stares are the final trigger to cause my knees to tremble furiously. Combined with the racing heart, the ringing ears and the ever-tightening chest, I know all too well that another panic attack is just moments away.

Desperately trying to keep it together to finish my speech, I blink repeatedly and try to regain the use of my tongue.

'I... I propose, in the aim of removing the stigma around mental health, we no longer think of the charity as Anxiety Anonymous, but as *Anxiety Together*. Because the very last thing anxiety should be is anonymous. No one should be dealing with anxiety and depression alone. We should be tackling the subject of mental health *together*.'

Struggling to place the microphone back into the holster, I gasp for breath as the crowd explodes into a series of cheers and whoops. In my haste to get away, I slip behind the black curtain and race down the steel steps, before sliding down to the ground when my legs give way beneath me. My gasps become louder as I try to stay in control, gaining the attention of the hired help by the speakers to my right.

'Are you alright?' One of the young lads asks, abandoning the wires he's holding and passing me a bucket. 'Do you need to be sick? Stage fright makes me nauseous, too.'

Taking the bucket from him, I manage a polite nod and place my head between my legs. I have to stay calm. I have to allow these feelings to happen without being afraid. Reminding myself of the grounding technique that has helped me so much in the past, I sit up straight and try to count five things I can see.

Stage... balloons... clouds... people... trees.

'Sadie!' Yvette squeals, clapping her hands together. 'Well done on your speech! Ruby was so proud! You were... Sadie? Are you okay?'

Stage... balloons... clouds... people... trees.

'Sadie?' Waving her hand in front of my face, Yvette beckons over Aldo. 'Aldo, something's wrong with Sadie.'

Shifting my focus to four things I can feel, I reach down to the ground and run my fingers through the blades of grass.

Grass... mud... bucket... wires.
Grass... mud... bucket... wires.

I can hear Aldo and Yvette reassuring me that everything will be okay, but the panic takes over and prevents me from responding. Covering my eyes with my hands, I try to concentrate on three things I can smell.

Doughnuts... an awful chemical scent from the portable loos behind us... Aldo's aftershave.

Repeating these three things over and over in my mind causes the tightening in my chest to slowly fade away as I block out the concerned babble from Yvette and Aldo and zone in on what else I can hear.

Birds chirping... children laughing.
Birds chirping... children laughing.
Birds chirping... children laughing.

Feeling my heart rate finally return to normal, I take one final deep breath before looking up again.

'Sorry about that.' I stammer, holding out my hand for Aldo to help me to my feet. 'I... I...'

'Was it the adrenaline? Did it get a bit much for you?' Yvette asks, passing me a bottle of water from her handbag. 'I'm exactly the same with public speaking. It gives me such a head rush.'

I take a sip of the water and brush my hair away from my damp face.

'Something like that...'

'Let's go and get you something to eat.' Giving me a concerned look, Aldo links my arm through his and hands the water bottle back to Yvette. 'You haven't eaten a thing all day. Your blood sugar has probably dropped.'

Smiling gratefully, I allow Aldo to lead me around the stage... and straight into a waiting Gavin Gastrell.

Chapter 16

Gavin's eyes burn into mine as I hold on to Aldo's arm to stop myself from falling to the ground. Only three minutes have passed since my last panic attack and if the feeling in my chest is anything to go by, I'm about to have another.

'Sadie...' Gavin begins, an expression on his face I can't quite read. 'Are you okay, love? You look a little pale.'

Seemingly losing the ability to speak, I stare back at Gavin open-mouthed. Paige, Mitch and Angela stand behind him, apparently unaware of who I am. I don't need to breathe a word to Aldo for him to know this man is my biological dad. The atmosphere is unbearably tense, making it impossible for him to be anyone else.

'I'm fine.' I reply, my voice wavering as I try to calculate what he is going to say next. 'How... how are you?'

'Good, thanks, love.' Pointing to his family, Gavin licks his lips nervously. 'I was just telling Angela all about you.'

'You were?'

I glance at a beaming Angela and worry that I'm going to vomit, but something tells me that informing his wife about the daughter he abandoned wouldn't result in such a warm smile.

'Yeah, she's been itching to put a face to the name ever since she found out I've been working down here.'

He says, not taking his eyes off mine. 'I told you I would bring her down, didn't I?'

'Yes, you did.' Feeling tears prick at the corner of my eyes, I move my gaze to Mitch and offer him a smile. 'Are you having a good time?'

'It's alright.' He replies quietly, momentarily looking up from his phone. 'The shooting range is pretty cool.'

'I'm guessing you won?' I ask, pointing to the fluffy bear under his arm. 'You must have a good aim. I don't think anyone else has managed to win anything.'

'I'm ashamed to say Paige won this.' Tossing the bear to his sister, he laughs with embarrassment. 'I didn't even come close.'

A tiny tear slips down my cheek and I desperately try to blink the rest back.

'Can I just say, I think you're amazing!' Paige gushes, her eyes lighting up as she speaks. 'Talking about your anxiety like that is so inspiring. You're so cool.'

'Very cool!' Angela adds, nodding in agreement. 'You're a fabulous role model for young girls. None of this lip filler and thigh gap nonsense. The world needs more people like you to show the younger generation the way. Mental health is such an important topic and events like this give it the platform it deserves. Well done, Sarah. You should be so very proud of yourself.'

'It's Sadie.' Gavin corrects, looking increasingly uneasy. 'Sadie Valentine.'

'Oh...' Angela giggles innocently and apologises. 'Like Shirley Valentine!'

'Exactly.' Aldo answers on my behalf. 'Our Shirley.'

Looking at the three kind faces in front of me, I feel my heart pang with sadness. I'm one of them and they have absolutely no idea.

'What's going on here?' A startled voice asks, breaking the spell with an alarmed gasp.

Turning around, I feel my blood run cold when I see my mum standing just inches behind us.

'Sadie? I said, *what's going on?*' The look of horror on her face makes my knees feel weak as I struggle to find something to say.

'Can you give us a moment?' She whispers to no one in particular, her face paling more with each second that passes. 'I need to talk to Sadie.'

As my mum walks towards me, Aldo squeezes my arm and I give him a nod which says he is fine to go. Clearly pre-empting the bombshell which is about to be revealed, Gavin tactfully guides his family towards the whack-a-mole station, leaving my mum and I completely alone behind the stage.

The noise of the fundraiser rings in my ears as she paces back and forth in front of me.

'I don't even know how to say this. I've been killing myself for days trying to find a way to put this into words without upsetting you, but I've still come up with a blank.' Her voice is thick with emotion as she exhales loudly and shakes her head. 'This is all my fault. I should have dealt with this before now. I should have put this to bed a very long time ago...'

Watching her torture herself, I stand perfectly still, feeling numb from head to toe.

'I don't know where to start...' She whispers, looking down at the ground and covering her mouth with her hand. 'Just know that the reason I didn't tell you is that I was protecting you. Protecting you was my main motivation and it always has been.'

Coming to a stop in front of me, she rests her hands on her hips and groans.

'Sadie, that man... the builder... he's...'

A whimper escapes her lips as she frantically tries to get her words out without crumbling.

'He's...'

'Mum, I know.' I interject, wrapping my arms around my body protectively. 'You don't have to do this.'

'I should have told you. I hate myself for not...' Her voice trails off as she registers what I have just said. 'What? You know what?'

'I know who he is.' I reply, not having the energy to pretend any longer. 'I know he's Gavin Gastrell. I know he's my dad.'

Her jaw drops open as she stares back at me in disbelief.

'But, how? How do you know that?'

Being very aware that we're in the middle of a huge swarm of people, I lower my voice and walk towards her.

'When I was a teenager, I asked about my dad and you gave me a name on a piece of paper. Do you remember?' She manages a tiny nod, all the while looking stunned into silence. 'Last year, I took it upon myself to put a face to the name.'

'No...'

'I found his address online and I drove to his home.'

'Oh, no...'

'He didn't know who I was and I didn't tell him. I just needed to see him for myself.' I say honestly, my heart beating harder with each word that tumbles out of my mouth. 'Even when he arrived at Blossom View with the contractors, it took me a few days to work out who he was. He just looked so different than I remembered. Maybe I blocked out our first meeting because it was so painful...'

Realising my mum has taken a seat on the bottom step of the ladders that lead back up to the stage, I follow her lead and sit down beside her.

'Until he saw you, he didn't have a clue who I was either. He must have put two and two together when you stumbled across one another in the kitchen that day.' I say carefully, becoming increasingly concerned by her reaction. 'If it makes you feel any better, I still don't think he knows that I know.'

'He's not your dad, Sadie.' She whispers, so quietly I can hardly hear her.

'What?' My brow crumples into a frown as I wait for her to respond. 'What are you talking about? Mum?'

Wiping tears from her cheeks, she rests her elbows on her knees.

'The truth is, Sadie, I don't know who your dad is. You kept pushing me and pushing me to tell you who he was and his was the only name I had...'

My mind goes into overdrive as I try to process what she is saying.

'I don't understand. You said... you said Gavin Gastrell was my dad...'

'I only said that because it was better than the reality!' She cries. 'I'm not proud of my behaviour, but

I was a little... *promiscuous* back then. We were just a couple of kids when Gavin and I dated. Being young and foolish, I told myself it was Gavin's baby I was carrying for no other reason than I wanted it to be. As the hospital appointments came and went, the midwife worked out the dates and you were almost impossible to be Gavin's.'

Her words hit me like a slap in the face, but I don't react. I just sit and listen to her say the things I have been waiting all of my life to hear.

'The other guy... I don't even know his name. I don't know where he lives. I don't know anything about him. I tried to hide the fact I was pregnant, but once I started showing it wasn't long before Gavin found out. I told him I wasn't sure who the father was and he freaked out. Like most teenage boys would. He left me high and dry and I've hated him for it ever since.' Finally looking at me, she shakes her head sadly. 'I'm sorry, Sadie, but the odds of Gavin being your father are little to none.'

'So, there's still a chance?' I ask, surprising myself with how okay I feel about this revelation.

'No...' She falters, seeming perplexed by my reaction. 'Well, maybe... I don't know.'

Maybe. My dad *may* be Gavin, or he *may* be someone whose name and location I'll never know. If I had a choice in how this pans out, I know which side of the coin I would be hoping for.

'I'm so sorry, Sadie...'

Lost in thought, I look up and spot Gavin walking our way. With his family preoccupied at the hook-a-duck stand, he trudges across the mud and stops a few feet in front of us.

'Linda, can I have a word?' He asks, his deep voice breaking slightly.

Scrambling to her feet, my mum wipes her damp eyes and grabs her handbag.

'Absolutely not!' She retorts angrily. 'You haven't tried to contact us once in all these years to find out if Sadie was your daughter. Don't you dare try to worm your way back into our lives now that we no longer need you!'

Roughly pushing past him, she races into the crowd without so much as looking back.

'I don't know what your mum told you about me, but please hear me out.' Gavin says, gently grabbing my arm as I attempt to run after her. 'Just five minutes, that's all I'm asking for.'

'You don't need to say anything.' I mumble, taking back my arm. 'There's nothing to say.'

'Are you kidding me? There's *everything* to say!' Sitting down on the step where my mum once sat, Gavin stuffs his hands in his pockets awkwardly. 'But the first thing is, I'm sorry. I've been sorry since the day I walked away from your mum. You just have to know that if I would have known, things would have been very different. If I would have known for sure that you were mine, I never would have left in the first place.'

'You don't need to explain yourself.' Tucking my hair behind my ears, I turn my face to the wind. 'You were just a kid yourself. Besides, we don't even know if you are my dad. From what my mum just told me, the odds aren't in your favour.'

'That's the thing, love.' Gavin whispers, placing a hand on my shoulder and removing it when I flinch.

'I've never known for certain. As the years went by, I told myself you weren't mine and moved on with my life, but if you *are*, I will do absolutely everything to make it up to you for being an absent father.'

A lump forms in the back of my throat and I furiously try to swallow it.

'But you have to understand that this could rip my family apart. They have no idea about any of this.' He says, his voice suddenly incredibly stern. 'I would need to know one hundred percent before I did that to them. You have to understand that?'

'Of course, I understand.' I say hurriedly, realising how serious this could become. 'You have your own life you need to protect.'

'I know this isn't any concern of yours, but I haven't exactly been the perfect husband to Angela over the years. Telling her I fathered a child I never told her about would probably be the straw that broke the camel's back.' Looking over at where his family are playing hook-a-duck, Gavin rubs his face agitatedly. 'I don't want to lose everything I've worked so hard to keep, but I give you my word. I'll take a test and if I'm your dad, we'll deal with it and I will take whatever it costs me on the chin.'

Completely numb to his words, I simply offer him a nod in response as he pushes himself up and starts to walk towards his family.

'One last thing.' He says, stopping and turning around to face me. 'If you knew who I was, why didn't you tell me? Why didn't you say anything straight away?'

I stare into the distance and allow my eyes to relax, until the throngs of people in front of me become a blurry haze.

'Because I knew that once I said it out loud it would become real and I didn't know if I wanted it to be.'

With a final sad smile, Gavin nods and walks away. Watching him fade into the crowd, I realise that despite today's events, I *still* don't know...

Chapter 17

'So, what happens now?' Aidan asks, from his position on the opposite end of the couch. 'Are you going to take a paternity test?'

'I don't know. Half of me wants to, but the other half is afraid of knowing.' Allowing my weight to sink into the cushions behind me, I twist my ring around my finger and shrug my shoulders.

'And his wife still doesn't have a clue?' Aldo asks in disbelief.

'Nope.' I reply, recalling the three beaming faces I was introduced to earlier. 'She has no idea at all...'

The fundraiser finished hours ago and ever since, Aidan, Aldo and I have been discussing the dramatic events that unfolded there at Blossom View. You would think that I'd be upset by the happenings with my mum and Gavin, but the truth is, I'm not, and that is what's unnerving me. I don't really know how I should react to this. Do I have any right to feel sad that Gavin most likely isn't my father after all? They say you can't lose something you never had, and in my case, that couldn't be truer. Gavin has *never* been in my life. The only thing that has changed for me is the name I kept in my purse all those years was a lie. The faded piece of paper should have been left blank, empty, like the role of a father in my life.

I did anticipate spending the night alone, torturing myself over my panic attack and the frankly disastrous goings-on earlier, but no sooner had the curtain fell at the fundraiser, both Aldo and Aidan insisted on walking me home. Seemingly putting his feelings towards Aidan to one side, Aldo hasn't sniped or made Aidan feel under the spotlight once. Looking at them now, as they make polite conversation in my living room, they actually seem to be getting along.

'Who are the lilies from?' Aldo asks, admiring the wilting box of lilies that have been stuffed behind the door. 'You do know flowers require watering, don't you?'

Reaching for the glossy box, he frowns and removes the ribbon.

'Honestly, Shirley, how you manage to keep fleabag alive when you can't be trusted to look after...'

'Leave them.' I reply curtly. 'They're from Spencer.'

Pausing with the lilies in his hands, Aldo pulls a pair of hairdressing scissors from his bag.

'Do you want me to cut the heads off them?'

'No!' Trying not to laugh, I confiscate his scissors and drop them on the coffee table. 'The flowers don't deserve their heads chopping off. It's not their fault.'

Reluctantly placing them back in the corner of the room, Aldo grabs some bottles of water from the fridge and tosses one to Aidan.

'If it's not the flowers fault, why don't you put them in water?' Aidan asks, giving the lilies a cursory glance.

'Because caring for them would indicate that I accept the gift and I most certainly do not.' I say quietly, running my fingers through Mateo's coat. 'Just ignore him and he will get the message... eventually.'

'So, you *do* have some brain cells rolling around in that tiny head of yours.' Aldo jokes. 'I did notice that he was cosying up to your mum before. Spencer, that is.'

'Spencer would cosy up to *anyone* if he thought it would put him at an advantage.' Rolling my eyes, I think back to being on the stage and seeing him with my mum and Mick. 'I don't hate her for falling for his charms. I've fallen for them enough times. He's an expert at playing people. He can squirm his way into your mind with a single smile and you would be none the wiser.'

'He certainly sounds quite the catch.' Aidan remarks.

'You don't know the half of it...' Clearing his throat, Aldo prepares himself to tell Aidan the whole Spencer story.

'And he doesn't need to!' I interject, shooting him a glare. 'Spencer and I are over. No number of lilies will ever change that.'

Aidan smiles back at me, before looking away when Aldo yawns loudly.

'On that note, I'm going home.' Aldo says suddenly, reaching for his jacket. 'Can I take the fleabag with me tonight?'

'Again?' I ask, straining my neck to look up at him. 'Why?'

A look of hurt flashes across Aldo's face and I immediately feel bad for questioning him.

'He likes it with me.' He insists. 'Besides, I think I saw a mouse a few nights back. Having him around will keep them at bay.'

'Okay, but you're going to have to stay by yourself sooner or later.' I say gently, holding out Mateo. 'I know Edward has only just gone, but you don't want to get into the habit of...'

'It's not about Edward.' He lies, cutting me off mid-sentence. 'It's about the mice, like I just said.'

Not wanting to embarrass him in front of Aidan, I take that as an end to the conversation and try to change the subject.

'What are you doing tomorrow?'

'Netflix and takeout...' He replies, without hesitating.

'Living on the wild side?' I tease.

'Well, what are you doing that's so exciting? Drinking Moet and swinging from the chandeliers?'

'Not exactly. I'm spending my Sunday helping Aidan with the barn conversion. He picked up the keys yesterday.'

'Congratulations!' Aldo says to Aidan, holding out his hand for a polite shake. 'Just don't let her near anything sharp, any power tools, or anything that requires more intelligence than is found in a baked bean.'

'Oi!' I laugh, batting him with a cushion. 'I think you will find my DIY is pretty good, actually.'

Looking over his shoulder, Aldo points to the wonky nest of tables by the fire and I feel my cheeks flush.

'Those were made using the heel of my stiletto as a hammer.' I protest with a scowl. 'Considering I had no tools or instructions, I think they have turned out pretty well!'

Aldo drops his wallet on one of the tables and we all laugh as it slides to the floor with a bang.

'How's *your* DIY?' Aidan asks, turning to face Aldo. 'I could do with an extra pair of hands, if you're at a loose end?'

Not wanting to admit that his DIY skills extend as far as painting his own nails when his beautician isn't free, Aldo pouts before replying.

'You're on.' He says decidedly, much to my delight. 'But I can't promise not to French manicure your skirting boards...'

Chapter 18

Sunday. The day of rest. Usually, I would be enjoying the day relaxing like most other people, but today, lounging in bed is the very last thing I would consider to be relaxing. Being alone with my thoughts is not somewhere I want to be right now. The truth is, I hardly slept a wink all night. As soon as the sun rose over the fields behind Blossom View, I threw back the duvet and scoured my wardrobe for the oldest clothes I could find.

Without so much as a glance in the mirror, I dived into the car and headed straight to Aldo's place. To my surprise, he was ready and waiting for me on the doorstep. I can't remember the last time I saw Aldo awake before eight o'clock on a weekend, but I'm sure it involved us stumbling back to our old apartment after a heavy night out in the village.

Looking at him now, as he carries building supplies into the barn with Aidan, I can't help thinking those laughter-filled nights feel so very far away. Sadness is carved into his pretty face in a way that makes my heart ache. I know all too well just how hard a breakup can hit a person and as much as he's trying to hide it, his sorrow is evident for everyone to see.

Watching the two of them disappear outside, I return to sweeping the pile of rubble in the living room and remark at how much better the place is looking. After just a few hours of elbow grease, the dilapidated barn is really coming together. It's going to take a heck of a lot of work to turn this into a home, but I can finally see what Aidan saw when we came to the viewing. Now that the dust is being blown away, what someone started before Aidan has been revealed. This was once a much-loved home, but over the years, the wear and tear has taken over and slowly destroyed what was here. In the same way that anxiety can take the shine and gloss off a person, time has disguised this as an abandoned building, when the reality runs much deeper.

With each shovel of rubbish I dump into the bin and with each bag of rubble I drag outside to the skip, I feel my anxiety gradually fade away. I've always been a big believer in the power of distraction, but today has really put the idea into practice. Witnessing the barn being brought back to life is giving me an overwhelming sense of achievement. Instead of obsessing over my problems, I am putting my time to better use. Being here with my two good friends is providing me with the comfort I am silently crying out for.

Carrying yet another bag of debris outside to the skip, I take a moment to soak up the sunshine and follow the sound of chatter to the garage behind the main building. I pause by the broken wooden doors and watch as Aldo and Aidan arrange an array of building supplies by the back wall. Pleased to see that they seem to be bonding, I start to head back to the barn when I hear my name mentioned.

'Shirley's great. She's my right-hand man, well, right-hand woman. I don't know what I would do without her...'

Smiling to myself, I revel in Aldo's kind words and brush my hair out of my face.

'I could say the same.' Aidan adds. 'Sadie saved me from a very bad place. I don't think I'll ever get over what happened, but if the meetings have taught me anything it's that time is the only thing against me now. Time is the only thing that helps.'

'Ironically, time is the one thing we have no control over.' Aldo replies, waiting for Aidan to pick up the other end of a workbench before dragging it across the garage. 'I've learnt that myself lately.'

'Yeah?'

Nodding back at him, Aldo curses loudly when he breaks a nail.

'I broke up with my boyfriend and it's hard to adjust to being on my own again. I haven't ever been on my own. Not really. I did have my own place for a while, but then I met Shirley and we lived together until I moved in with Edward. The feeling of being completely alone is awful.'

A pang of sadness hits me as I listen to Aldo speak. I knew he was finding it difficult without Edward. Aldo's always hated being in his own company. When we shared the apartment, we were together twenty-four hours a day and I would be lying if I said I didn't miss that time in our lives, but learning to love himself is a lesson Aldo is going to have to learn on his own.

'I feel for you.' Aidan sighs, pausing to wipe his brow before reaching for a bag of cement. 'I suppose what you're feeling is a little like grief.'

'Comparing it to grief makes me feel pathetic. I mean, you've been through so much and you're still standing. I just need to pull myself together.'

'You shouldn't say that.' Aidan says seriously. 'Grief affects us on all different levels. If you're feeling low, you should speak to Sadie.'

'I don't like to go to Shirley with stuff like this. I'm the strong one in our friendship. *I've* always looked after *her*. The way she was last year... I'll never forget it. I don't want to let her down.'

'From how highly Sadie speaks of you, I don't think you could ever let her down.' Aidan replies. 'We all need a shoulder to cry on from time to time.'

'I guess so. I just don't like talking about *feelings* or any of that stuff.' Aldo admits. 'Guys don't, do we?'

Shaking his head, Aidan takes off his gloves and perches on the edge of the pallet.

'We don't and that's the dangerous thing. As men, we have this tendency to think that we have to be macho and strong. That we aren't allowed to display emotion in case it is perceived as a weakness, but we don't have to be brave all the time. Men have just as much right as women to admit that they're, you know, having a hard time upstairs.'

Peeking around the door once more, I spot Aldo nodding in agreement.

'Breakups are always tough.' Aidan continues. 'It's completely normal to feel the way you're feeling after ending a relationship, but from my experience, I only started to feel better once I admitted I needed a helping hand. Like I said before, speak to Sadie.'

'I just need some time on my own to get my head around things, but I take your point.' Folding his arms, Aldo kicks up a pile of dust and shrugs his shoulders. 'I know my limits and I'll reach out if things get too much...'

Slowly retreating back into the barn, I sigh heavily and reach for the sweeping brush. It seems we're all fighting a battle. No matter how big or small. Even those you think are built of steel will have that one thing that can cause them to feel just two inches tall, but Aidan is right. Men *do* have a tough time when it comes to looking after their mental health. The taboo surrounding mental health in general is slowly fading away, but where men are concerned, we still have a fair way to go.

I've always believed that small changes can lead to huge transformations and I'm confident that with time, we *can* change the attitude towards men's mental health. Because a tiny change is really all it takes. A tiny change in the minds of many people isn't just how we move forward, it's how we change the entire world...

Chapter 19

Making my way down the stairs, I pause in the hallway and fasten my watch to my wrist. With Jason and his team due to arrive at any moment, I intend to make my escape before, or rather *if*, Gavin makes an appearance. The sound of my heels on the wooden floorboards echoes around the empty cottage as I twist my hair into a messy bun at the nape of my neck. After overhearing Aldo's conversation at the barn yesterday, I decided to let him keep Mateo for another night. We all cope with the demise of a relationship in our own way and if Mateo's company is what Aldo needs to help him through, so be it.

Ironically, being completely alone is exactly what I craved. When I arrived back at Blossom View yesterday, I hid myself away from everything and everyone. I turned off my phone, closed the curtains and slipped beneath the duvet. I know taking cover from the world isn't going to make my problems go away, but the truth is, I couldn't face anyone. I just needed a single evening to myself.

Learning to be alone with my problems is one of the most difficult lessons I have learnt along the way. I don't need reassurance and I don't need someone to tell me that everything will be okay. Because if the past twelve months have taught me anything, it's that if it's not okay, it's not the end. It *will* pass and I shall soon be looking back on this time and kicking myself for allowing my negative thoughts to ruin my peace.

What will be, will be, regardless of how much time I commit to worrying about things and wishing they were different. I can't change the future and I can't change the past. I just have to live in the present and make it the best it can possibly be, which is exactly why I am up, dressed and ready to flee the house before my main problem arrives.

Tossing my phone into my handbag, I step outside and close the front door behind me. The blue skies we have been enjoying lately are covered in a blanket of grey cloud, causing a cold wind to whip around my body as I trudge down the garden path.

'Sadie!' A gruff voice hollers in the distance. 'Morning, Sadie, love!'

My stomach drops to the floor as I look up to see Jason and his bevy of builders speeding my way in his van. With a polite wave, I manage a thin smile and race to the car in the hope I can get away before they get out of the van, but no sooner have I put the key in the ignition, a worried looking Gavin knocks gently on the bonnet.

Trying not to panic, I lower the window and bite my lip as his eyes dart around nervously.

'I just wanted to give you this.' He whispers, holding out a white envelope with a shaky hand. 'I've already done my part.'

Accepting the envelope from him, I notice the address and gulp. *O.L.E DNA Testing, London, SW2 1CC.*

'You don't have to take it.' Keeping his voice hardly above a whisper, he wipes a bead of sweat from his forehead. 'I probably should have asked you first before I... before I...'

'No, it's okay.' I reply, slipping the envelope into the glove compartment. 'You really didn't have to take a test...'

'Of course, I bloody had to!' Gavin interrupts, almost tearfully. 'If... if you *are* my daughter, I will spend the rest of my life making it up to you. That is, if you want me to?'

Staring back at him, I look into his eyes and try to answer his question. Do I want him to make it up to me? Do I want this man to take the role of dad in my life? Do I want him in my life *at all?* I could hand him back the envelope, wait for him to finish working on the cottage and continue with my life. I've made it this far without a father, why change things now? Why risk jumping out of the frying pan and into the fryer? If this test proves that Gavin Gastrell is my father, what happens next? Will I be welcomed into his family, or do I sit back and watch his family fall apart?

Knowing there's a whole lot more riding on this than a simple cheek swab, I clear my throat and start the engine.

'I have to go.' I say quietly, fastening my seatbelt and reaching for the handbrake. 'I'm going to be late for work... as are you.'

Gavin's lips slowly curl into a tiny small as he nods and steps away from the car.

'Good point. Have a good day, love.'

'You too.'

Waiting for him to retreat to the van, I start the car and turn on the radio. I should be pleased. I should be overjoyed by Gavin's response to this bombshell. Within forty-eight hours, this man has risked his entire future by taking a test that could change his life forever. He is pledging to be the father I never had, regardless of being told the odds are stacked against him. So, why do I feel so *nothing* about it? A tiny part of me would have preferred him to have walked away from this. In a way, it would be so much easier than the whole gamble of just not knowing. The outcome would be guaranteed. I wouldn't have to make a choice. I wouldn't have to make a decision that could lead to a whole new world of pain.

Glancing at the glove compartment, I turn up the radio in a bid to drown out my thoughts. They say you should listen to your mind when it whispers, so that you won't have to hear it scream, but what if the whisper is telling you something you're not sure you want to hear?

*   *   *

Smiling at the many faces staring back at me, I hold my identification card in my hands and take a deep breath before speaking.

'This past week has reminded me that sometimes in life, anxiety is a normal feeling to experience. Because the truth is, life isn't always a bed of roses. Anxiety is only a problem when it becomes excessive and due to the fact that you're all here today, I'm going to assume you're already aware of that. When you have a history of anxiety, it's easy to misinterpret an occasion where anxiety is a completely normal reaction as a relapse. It's important to understand the difference between relapsing and experiencing a normal emotion. How you choose to react to the anxiety is what separates the two.'

Recalling how I've been feeling over the past couple of weeks makes my tummy flip, but I believe it is important for the support group to hear this.

'Learning to control how we react to anxiety is something that takes patience and perseverance, but just because we stumble doesn't mean that we have to fall. Don't kick yourself for having a wobble. Don't allow a minor incident to undo the mountain of work you have put into your journey back to mental wellness. The only thing you can measure your success against, is how you would have dealt with a situation at the very start of this process.'

A mumble comes back at me from the circle of attendees and I shuffle my seat a little closer.

'It's easy to think you haven't come far, or that not much has changed for you, but the next time you feel that anxiety is creeping into your life, just cast your mind back to how you would have reacted to that feeling this time last week, month or year. I think, no, I *know*, you will be impressed by how much you have progressed.'

I move my gaze from one person to the next, until I have locked eyes with everyone in the support group.

'I have had to do exactly that over the past few days. I've been tested with a couple of situations that this time last year would have sent me spiralling into a black hole, but I didn't. For the majority of the time, I have managed to keep the control. Yes, I've been faced with instances where I would previously have crumbled and allowed anxiety to nibble away at me. Yes, I have been scared, felt afraid, alone and every other awful emotion that comes with it. However, when I first walked through those doors, the things I've dealt with this week would have broken me. They would have sent me right back to my darkest days, but because of being here, because of implementing the techniques I have learnt along the way, I have managed to keep moving forward.'

'That's fantastic, Sadie.' Alec says enthusiastically. 'Well done.'

'Thanks, Alec, but I'm not looking for praise.' I say quickly, realising I've been talking about myself for the last twenty minutes. 'I just wanted to share with you that I still struggle with my anxiety. It takes so much courage for you all to confide your struggles in me, and I simply sit here and try to advise you the best I can. But I want you to know that being on the other side of the circle doesn't mean anxiety doesn't affect me. It simply means I am equipped to deal with it when it hits...'

An image of myself crawling through the door here, filled with angst and panic jumps into my mind and I am hit with an immense sense of pride. Pride for how well I am dealing with everything and pride for having the ability to recognise it.

Blinking back a couple of happy tears, I cross my legs and get settled in my seat.

'Anyway, that's enough from me. Let's talk about all of you...'

THE KEY TO HAPPINESSS IS FREEDOM.
THE KEY TO FREEDOM IS COURAGE.

Chapter 20

Panting for breath, I grab a bottle of water from the fridge and frantically unscrew the cap. My head throbs as I lean against the cold counter and try to steady my breathing. What started as a brisk stroll quickly escalated to a high-impact sprint. Pounding my feet against the pavement made my lungs burn and my legs ache, but each step I took cleared my mind a little more.

I hoped the open air of the forest would enable me to think more clearly and it did, to an extent. Being away from the hustle and bustle of daily life gave me the space to forget about the rest of the world for a while, but it wasn't the magic pill I was searching for. I didn't have a light-bulb moment, where the answer to my problems popped into my head like in the movies, and I didn't leave feeling rested and rejuvenated. I did, however, achieve a strange sense of calmness. A calmness in that I might not have the answers just yet, but I am ready to start searching for them.

Kicking off my mud-covered trainers, I open the back door and follow the path to the iron bench at the bottom of the garden. The blossom tree hangs beautifully overhead, casting the seat in a cooling shadow as I sit down and take the white envelope out of my pocket. Crisp green leaves surround me and I cast my mind back to when the same tree was in full bloom. Delicate pink flowers flooded the garden just a few short months ago, now they are nowhere to be seen. Like a figment of my imagination, a memory and nothing more, until the seasons change and it springs to life once again.

That's the frustrating thing about life. We don't know the true value of a moment until it becomes a mere memory. We also don't know if what we're worrying about today will still matter once it *becomes* a memory. Time is the only thing that will tell and as I have been reminded so much lately, time is the only thing we cannot change.

Picking up the envelope, I reach inside and pull out the letter for the first time. The words on the page cause my stomach to churn uncontrollably. *Paternity... accurate... results... guaranteed... fast.* Just a cheek swab. That's all it will take to put the question mark over my biological father to bed forever. Taking out one of the plastic tubes, I squint at the handwritten label and realise that Gavin has already filled it in. His clumsy handwriting spreads out of the designated box. Messy, awkward and untidy. Just like my own.

Tipping my head back, I look out over the fields in the distance. The sun is starting to set, resulting in a beautiful display of burnt orange in the sky ahead. Hearing Mateo's bell chime as he jumps up and joins me on the bench, I smile down at him when he curls up on my lap.

'It's been a funny old day, Mateo.' I whisper, hoping that my neighbours can't hear me. 'No matter which way you look at it, it's been a funny old day indeed...'

My speech at the support group earlier comes flooding back to me as I look at the envelope once more. It *does* matter which way you look at things. It matters massively. Rather than dwelling on how this past couple of weeks have made me succumb to panic attacks, I should be celebrating the fact that unlike last year, I have made it through the rough patch and out the other side. I haven't allowed the anxiety to beat me. I have stayed strong. I have held it together. I have made it through.

Watching darkness fall over the garden, I'm reminded that the only reason I've dealt with things differently is because of the help I've received along the way. Being introduced to Anxiety Anonymous is what made me realise I had the strength to stand up to my anxiety, and the guys at the support group are who gave me the courage to use it.

When humans come together, we really can beat anything. The power generated by people uniting as one is unparalleled. Alone we are weak, together we are strong. Problems become opportunities when we join forces and it's quite magical to witness. Anxiety Anonymous is an incredible charity. It's a charity that helps the lives of so many people, but anonymous it certainly isn't. The support group brings sufferers together and reassures them they're not alone in their battle with anxiety. Just like I said at the fundraiser, we shouldn't think of the charity as *Anxiety Anonymous*, we should think of it as *Anxiety Together*.

The sun finally slips out of sight, leaving Mateo and I sitting in complete darkness, but a light switches on inside me. Anxiety is always going to be a problem for people, as people will always have problems, but as long as we keep campaigning for those suffering, things can only get better. After my first bout of anxiety, I decided I wanted to use my experience to help others who have been through the same battle, so why stop at counselling the support group? I don't just want to help the residents of Wilmslow and its neighbouring villages through anxiety, I want to help everyone, *everywhere*. Even if it's in the smallest way possible, I want to make an impact that's going to change the world for the better.

Julia once told me that every altercation with anxiety is an opportunity to test just how strong we really are and that's exactly what I intend to do. My dilemma over Gavin Gastrell isn't going anywhere, but while I figure it out, I'm going to use my time to put mental health on the map. People look up to me at the meeting, so I'm going to give them something to really look up to. I won't allow anxiety to control my life or anyone else's without a fight. Sunsets are proof that no matter what happens to ruin your day, every day *can* end beautifully, you just have to open your eyes and look.

Placing Mateo on the floor, I head into the living room and take a notepad from the drawer in the coffee table. It's been a while since I made an Unhappiness List, but unlike last time, I know exactly what to put on it. My pen scrawls against the page effortlessly as I quickly scribble down the same three things again and again. Regardless of what the list contains, the end goal is the same. Address what requires change and formulate a plan to change it. Sounds easy in principle, doesn't it? And I guess the first part is, but fixing these issues is a whole other ball game. After all, if we knew how to fix our problems, there wouldn't be any problems in the first place.

There was a time when my Unhappiness List contained just one thing. *Be happy.* I remember writing those two little words as though it was just yesterday. Back then, simply being happy seemed so very hard to achieve. It took me a long time to realise that being happy is a basic human right. It also took me a long time to understand that it's okay to want more than that. It's not a crime to dream bigger, or to have a desire to leave your imprint on the planet in a way that changes the world in some way. I'm not talking about curing cancer, finding world peace or starting life on Mars, but if you *can* make a change, if you *are* able to make the world a better place, then why not? What's stopping you?

My skin prickles with excitement as I draw a line beneath my completed list. Pouring my problems onto the page makes my shoulders feel ten pounds lighter. When you have so many thoughts racing through your mind, it's virtually impossible to organise them. Writing your issues down makes them more real somehow. It brings them to life in a way that makes you believe you can fix them.

Tearing the page from the notepad, I wander out into the garden once more and return to the bench. The envelope containing the paternity test is exactly where I left it. Placing the Unhappiness List on top of it, I look up at the sky and notice how it is now speckled with glistening stars. Some dazzle more than others, some have a tinge of yellow and others are hardly visible at all. As I move my eyes across the sky, I single out one star that is outshining the rest. It's bigger, brighter and breathtakingly stunning.

Stars have always given me a sense of hope. They tease of a promise that something incredible is waiting just around the corner. No matter what cards you are dealt, no matter what life decides to try you with, the stars will still be there, lighting up the sky with a million diamonds. A million sparkling promises that something better is coming, you just have to wade through the darkness to see them...

Chapter 21

They say when you don't know where to start, start at the top and work your way down, which is exactly what I have done. The moment I opened my eyes this morning, I bit the bullet and tackled the first thing on my list head-on. Pushing the rest of my Unhappiness List to the back of my mind was not an easy task, but as I sit opposite Julia in the Anxiety Anonymous offices, I just know I have made the right choice.

'Well, it's certainly an interesting idea, Sadie.' She says thoughtfully, brushing back her greying curls and pursing her lips. 'Very interesting...'

The idea she is referring to came to me last night. As I looked up at the stars, the thought hit me like a lightning bolt. The change I was searching for to help people with anxiety suddenly seemed so obvious. Like it had been staring me in the face all along. It's just one word. One word with so much meaning.

'When did you think of this?' Pushing her glasses up the bridge of her nose, Julia taps her fingers on the side of the armchair. 'It's just that... *Anxiety Together?* I'm sure I've heard that somewhere before...'

'It was at the fundraiser.' I explain, quietly overjoyed that she remembered. 'In my speech, I mentioned that we shouldn't be associating anxiety with anonymity. We should be promoting an idea of togetherness. We need to fight anxiety as one unit, as one family.'

Nodding in response, Julia appears to be deep in thought. With her brow creased into a frown, she stares at the vase of flowers in the middle of the table intently. She could have shut my idea down immediately and a huge chunk of me thought she would, but she hasn't. She simply listened without interrupting as I reeled off my hastily-prepared proposal. There's nothing more I can do now. I just need to bide my time and wait for her reply...

'The ethos behind changing the name is truly remarkable.' She says finally, bringing her eyes up to mine. '*Anxiety Together*. It's exactly the message we want to send out. I can't believe I haven't thought of it myself.'

'I knew you would agree!' Not being able to stop myself from grinning manically, I clap my hands together with glee. 'The idea hit me last night and it just made so much sense...'

'Sadie...' Holding up her hand to silence me, Julia leans back in her seat. 'Let's not get too excited here.'

The tone of her voice gives me a reality check and I feel my smile drop slightly.

'I agree that changing the name would portray our message a lot clearer than it currently does. Speaking out about mental health is our primary mission statement and anything that aids that is obviously a huge plus.' Tipping her head to one side, she fiddles with one of her earrings and sighs. 'However, changing the name of a charity as big as Anxiety Anonymous is not an easy task, by any stretch of the imagination. The charity has dozens of branches across the country and as such, it has built up such a recognisable brand...'

'Maybe a rebrand is exactly what the charity needs.' I blurt out, in a bid to dispel her argument. 'Anxiety is huge news at the moment. It's everywhere you look. Mental health is finally in the spotlight after years of being swept under the rug. Celebrities are talking about it, men are coming forward with their struggles... it's even being discussed in parliament. People everywhere are standing up to the once taboo subject of mental health. This is our chance to jump on board the ship and put the charity on the map.'

Responding with nothing more than a solemn stare, Julia signals for me to continue.

'Just think how amazing it would be to do our bit to remove the stigma around matters of the mind. We have both been on the receiving end of anxiety and we both know how difficult it is to reach out for help.' I pause for breath and allow her a moment to digest my argument. 'Just imagine a support group that goes against everything we already know about support groups. Let's remove the idea of a bleak room where people hide in the shadows, too afraid to reveal their name because they're worried about what others will think. Instead, picture a support group with a difference. Picture a place where strangers become friends and friends become family. Picture a place that talks loud and proud about anxiety. Picture a place that completely revolutionizes the whole philosophy of support groups. That place you are picturing is *Anxiety Together...*'

My words trail into silence as I realise Julia is smiling back at me. It's not a polite little smile. It's a smile that makes her eyes sparkle like gemstones.

'You know what I think, Sadie?' She whispers, her voice high with excitement. 'I think you're a breath of fresh air. You are exactly what this charity needs.'

'I am?'

'Yes, you are. You're young, energetic, vibrant and brimming with new ideas.' Placing her hands in her lap, Julia grins widely. 'I'll speak to the powers that be...'

A gasp escapes my lips and I clasp my hands over my mouth.

'Don't get your hopes up.' Julia warns sternly. 'If they were to go for it, and that is one big if, it would take a very long time to implement. However, I genuinely believe you are on to something here...'

My heart races as I listen to her speak. This is it! The ball is officially rolling! The wheels are in motion...

'How would you feel about pitching this to the board with me?' She asks suddenly, causing my stomach to sink. 'You did such a marvellous job at the fundraiser. People really seem to relate to you.'

Not wanting to lie to her, I shake my head sadly.

'I have to tell you that I struggled with the speech at the fundraiser.' I say honestly, looking down at the ground as I recall looking out over the sea of people. 'When I came off the stage, I had a panic attack...'

'You did?' Julia exclaims in surprise. 'Sadie, I'm so sorry to hear that. If I thought for one second it would give you a panic attack, I would never have allowed you to get up there.'

Shaking off her apology, it takes me all of thirty seconds to realise that my desire to help the charity outweighs my fear of another panic attack.

'But...' I continue, beaming confidently. 'I'll do it anyway.'

'Really? Are you sure?'

'The charity saved my life and for that, I will forever be in its debt.' Glancing at my finger tattoo, I recall my Unhappiness List and take a deep breath. 'Whatever it takes to make this happen, you can count me in.'

'And that mentality, Sadie Valentine, is exactly why we need you...'

*   *   *

Jumping into the car, I wait until the door closes behind me before letting out an ear-piercing squeal. I've done it. I've actually done it! Well, not quite, but I've done exactly what I set out do. Not only is Julia keen on the idea, she's arranged a time, date and location for an official pitch to take place. A surge of adrenaline rushes through my veins as I bang my hand on the steering wheel with joy.

With my Unhappiness List in my handbag, I am suddenly in control. I have the power to change the things I can and accept the things I can't. It's incredibly liberating. Allowing myself a few moments to absorb the sense of immense satisfaction, I snap back to attention when my phone rings from its resting place in the centre console.

Squinting at the screen, I smile when I see Ruby's name pop up on the display.

'*Hello?*' I sing, shaking the handset as I'm greeted with a plain black screen. 'Ruby? Are you there?'

A few seconds later, the display springs to life and my friend pops up in front of me.

'Hey!' She grins, waving at the camera happily. 'How are you?'

'I'm good!' Glancing over my shoulder at the Anxiety Anonymous offices behind me, I feel a frisson of excitement. 'I'm *really* good. How are you?'

'I've been trying to call you since the fundraiser, but you haven't returned my calls?' Ruby says accusingly, choosing to ignore my question. 'What's going on?'

'I'm sorry about that. I've been meaning to call you back, it's just that things have been a little... *weird* around here lately.'

'Define weird?' She demands, staring into the camera. 'Good weird or bad weird?'

'Right now, good weird, but it has been bad weird and everything in between.' Looking at my handbag out of the corner of my eye, I debate telling Ruby about Gavin, but something inside me decides against it. 'Anyway, that's enough about me. How have you been?'

Narrowing her eyes at the screen, Ruby flips her hair over her shoulder and scowls.

'We both know I'm not going to leave it at *weird...* because you know, that would be *weird.*'

I let out a laugh and shake my head. Ruby always knows when I'm hiding something, but I really don't want to burden her with everything that has happened. Not because I can't face going over it again, but simply because I don't want to worry her.

'It's a long story, Ruby. A long story that isn't quite over yet, but I promise you that everything is going to be just fine.'

Sensing the tone, she reluctantly accepts this and nods.

'So, what's been going on with you?' I ask, desperate to hear about her latest adventure. 'How's island life?'

'Fabulous.' Holding up a backpack, she points to a yellow Jeep in the background. 'We're going on a nature trail today. Our tour guide, Joseph, promises it will leave us with a sense of spiritual enlightenment.'

'That sounds exciting.'

'It is, but that isn't why I was calling you. I thought you would like to know that I have been flying the flag for Anxiety Anonymous over here.' She says proudly, resting her chin on her backpack. 'I told you before about a couple of the other girls being homesick, didn't I?'

I nod in response as I recall our previous conversation.

'Well, it turns out they were more than a little homesick. One of the girls, Poppy, had made the decision to go home because she was feeling so low. It was then that I had a brainwave.' Ruby explains with a grin. 'I overheard her talking to one of the others about how anxious she was feeling and I just thought, she needs to speak to Julia, or you, or just anyone from the support group. Then I realised that *I* am someone from the support group. So, I took it upon myself to start a little support group of my own.'

'You did?' I exclaim, feeling an enormous sense of pride. 'That's fantastic! I'm so proud of you.'

'I thought you would be.' Her eyes sparkle happily as she grins back at me. 'There are five of us now and we meet down on the beach each night to watch the sunset. I felt a bit awkward at first, you know, with not being a counsellor or anything, but I was surprised by how much I knew, and I was even more surprised by how much it helped them.'

Reaching into her pocket, Ruby produces a tiny handwritten thank you card.

'Poppy left this on my pillow this morning and it got me thinking. Some cases of anxiety are so easily treated. Having someone to talk through your problems with is one of the best remedies there is. Just knowing that you're not alone is so powerful. We know how anxiety preys on those who feel lonely, but when people come together, amazing things can happen.'

The hairs on the back of my neck stand on end as I repeat that last sentence in my mind.

When people come together, amazing things can happen.

'Do you believe in fate, Ruby?' I ask, as a wave of inspiration hits me. 'Because I'm going to need your help...'

Chapter 22

With my conversation with Julia still fresh in my mind, I returned to Blossom View firing on all cylinders. In the space of a few shorts hours, I have created a vision board of ideas on the back of a roll of wallpaper. My thoughts come thick and fast as I move along the paper, desperately trying to keep up with the ideas that are screaming to be heard in my mind, demanding to be given a voice.

Once I am confident I'm done, I drop the pen and sit cross-legged on the carpet to admire my handiwork. The aftermath of my brainwave is splattered across the unravelled roll of paper in front of me. Like a firework that has messily exploded and missed its mark, the indecipherable splodges read like the ramblings of a crazy person, but to me, they make perfect sense. It begins with an explanation of my arrangement with Ruby and continues to a map of potential places to start a petition in favour of the name change. The map leads to a list of people I can ask for references regarding how much the charity has helped them. Said list is much longer than I thought it would be, with name after name covering the paper like a series of chaotic autographs.

Moving along the carpet, I come to a picture that makes my heart leap. In a scrappily drawn house, a whole bunch of tiny stickmen stand shoulder to shoulder. Smiles are on all of their faces, causing me to automatically grin back. The charity logo is emblazoned on the roof, but it's not the logo as we know it. My impromptu version of an Anxiety Together logo is a world away from the traditional black and white logo of Anxiety Anonymous. Using all the colours of the rainbow, my interpretation uses the *t* in anxiety to form a vertical *together* and finishes with yet another smiley face in the *o*.

Tearing my eyes away from the roll of paper that is cluttering the living room floor, I remember that Aldo shall be here at any moment. Since I overheard his conversation with Aidan at the weekend, it has taken all my willpower not to drive over to his house. I want to demand he opens up to me over a bottle of fizz and a greasy pizza, but my training for the support group taught me that you can't force someone to talk to you. Doing so will only result in them retreating further into their shell. I simply have to let him know I am there for him.

Hearing a knock at the door, I don't have time to get up before Aldo's voice travels down the hallway.

'Shirley?'

'In here!' I reply, looking up as Aldo steps into the living room with Mateo trailing behind him. 'You look amazing!'

His long hair is twisted into his trademark bun at the top of his head, without a single hair out of place. He's wearing his favourite *pulling* jeans and a shirt so tight, you would believe it was painted on.

'I *always* look amazing.' Flashing me a grin, he tosses his car keys onto the couch as Mateo pads across the carpet to greet me. 'I would say the same, but you know how I feel about those dungarees.'

Ignoring his playful jibe, I pull Mateo onto my lap and twirl his tail around my finger.

'Have you missed me?' I sing happily, as he rubs his nose against mine. 'Yes, you have! Yes, you have! Yes, you have!'

'You've got mail.' Aldo interrupts, holding out a letter. 'It was on the mat.'

Taking the note from him, I squint at the writing and frown.

'Oh, it's from Jason. The guy who has been...'

'I know who you mean. What does it say?'

'It says they should soon be done here.' I reply, slipping the note into my pocket. 'In just a few days, apparently.'

'And he couldn't text you and say that? Or, you know, call?' Aldo scoffs. 'What year is this guy living in, 1802?'

Smiling at finally hearing Aldo's wit return, I shrug my shoulders in response. The truth is, Jason's not texting or calling because he's tried to, but I haven't answered his attempts to contact me. Since I was presented with the paternity test, I've made a conscious effort to never be in the same room as Gavin, Jason, or any of the other builders. It's so much easier to pretend they don't exist while I decide what I am going to do about it. Just like the dozens of calls I've ignored from my Mum, and the many, *many* bouquets of flowers I've refused to sign for from Spencer.

'Erm, my phone's been playing up.' I lie, scratching the tip of my nose. 'I'll deal with it later. I have my hands full right now...'

'I can see that.' Sitting on the floor next to me, he pulls the wallpaper towards him. 'What the hell happened in here?'

'This is the result of my brainstorming session...'

'Looks more like brain vomit to me.'

'It's not brain vomit!' I giggle, relieved to see my friend back to his sarcastic best. 'This is research for what could be the biggest presentation I will ever give...'

As I bring Aldo up to speed on the amazing opportunity I've been given, I notice how my stomach churns wildly. First with nerves, then with fear and finally with the belief that I could actually make this happen.

'Wow, Shirley!' Aldo exclaims. 'That's incredible!'

'I know. I just don't want to mess it up.'

'You won't mess it up!' Turning the roll of paper around to face him, Aldo smiles at the Anxiety Together logo. 'Is there anything I can do to help?'

'I was hoping you would say that! If I'm going to pull this off, I'm going to need as many hands on deck as possible.'

'Well, you can count me in.' He replies easily. 'I'd do anything to help with anxiety, Shirley, and anything for you.'

'Ditto.' I say with a grin, resisting the urge to squeeze him. 'Whatever you need, anything, just make your voice known.'

'What does that mean?' Picking up my pen, he sketches a French braid in the corner of the wallpaper roll.

'Nothing!' I stammer, not wanting to make things awkward. 'It's just that... it's just that I know things must be pretty rubbish for you right now. If you need to talk or are feeling down, please don't keep it bottled up. I know you like to be macho, manicures and spray tans aside, but you don't have to be. I'm always here.'

Not looking up from his sketch, Aldo taps his pen on the paper slowly.

'Thanks, Shirley, but I'm doing alright now.' He says honestly, stretching out his legs as Mateo jumps onto his lap. 'When Edward left, I panicked. I completely freaked out. The reality of being on my own hit me harder than I expected, but these past couple of days have made me realise why I ended it in the first place. Edward was great, but he's not what I want right now. I need to learn to be on my own and he needs to concentrate on his career. Right guy, wrong time. It happens.'

Studying his face as he strokes Mateo, I find myself nodding in agreement.

'I think you're right.' I reply seriously. 'Concentrating on number one for a while will be really good for you.'

'That's what Aidan said. Word for word.'

'Aidan?' I repeat, my heart starting to beat a little faster.

'Yeah, I've been at the barn with him these past few days.' Taking his phone from his pocket, he presents his me with some pictures of the barn renovations. 'Talking to Aidan is what made me see sense.'

Unable to hide how shocked I am, I feel my jaw drop open as he flicks through the gallery.

'*You've* been at the barn with Aidan?'

'Is there something wrong with your ears?'

'No.' I stutter, giving his phone a fleeting glance. 'I'm just surprised, that's all. I thought you didn't like him.'

'I got him wrong.' Aldo admits, stretching his arms over his head. 'I told him the same last night. We went for a drink at The Shepard and had a great talk. He made me see the reasons I ended the relationship in the first place...'

Completely lost for words, I stare at my good friend as he continues to wax lyrical about Aidan.

'He was asking about you.' He says suddenly, looking at me with an expression I can't quite decipher. 'He said you know where he is if you need a friend...'

My mind jumps back to the daisy that is safely tucked behind a photo of Mateo in my bedroom. I should have called him, but with having so much on my plate right now, I didn't have the energy for anything or anyone else.

'Why don't you go over there?' Aldo continues, obviously reading my mind. 'He'd be happy to see you. Delighted, in fact.'

'I could do.' Butterflies attack my tummy and I bite my lip nervously. 'Do you want to come with me?'

'You think these were made for a damn barn?' Pointing to his white jeans, Aldo feigns horror.

'Fair point.' I reply, holding out a hand to help him to his feet. 'What do you have planned? Where are you going from here?'

Smoothing down his shirt, Aldo raises an eyebrow and turns to face the mirror. A wicked smile plays on his lips as he winks at his reflection.

'Do you really want to know?'

Knowing that Aldo's pre-Edward days consisted of him doing tequila shots from the crotches of very beautiful men, I shake my head in response.

'As long as you are happy, Aldo, I really don't...'

Chapter 23

I probably should have called Aidan first, or at least sent him a text, but I foolishly told myself it would be fun to surprise him. My impulsive side convinced me that spontaneity would be a good idea. Now that I am here, I am starting to question my decision. Breathing deeply, I pause outside the barn to smooth down my hair before pushing open the heavy door. The old hinges squeak loudly as I step inside the building, making me feel like an intruder as I try to navigate my way around the barn.

Following the sound of laughter, I grimace when the door bangs behind me. The laughter stops for a moment before becoming even louder than it was before. Tracing the voices, I walk through the makeshift dining room and discover Aidan in the kitchen.

'Sadie!' He beams, leaning against the breakfast bar that wasn't there the last time I was here. 'It's so great to see you!'

'It's great to see you, too.' My lips spring into a smile and I tuck my hair behind my ears coyly. 'I was meaning to call you.'

Taking a step towards him, my smile falters when I notice Frankie standing by the window.

'Hey!' She says, her blindingly-white teeth gleaming as she grins at me widely.

'Hi, Frankie.' Completely floored at discovering her here, I look back at Aidan before returning my focus to her. 'What are you doing here?'

Flipping her hair over her shoulder, Frankie drapes an arm around Aidan's shoulder and positions her face next to his.

'I'm hitting Aidan with my best sweet-talking.' She purrs, giving his shoulders a quick rub. 'I've been working him all day.'

'Oh...' Suddenly feeling incredibly stupid for coming over here uninvited, I slip my sleeves over my hands self-consciously. 'I can come back, if it's a bad time?'

Giggling like a teenager, Frankie shakes her head and totters around the breakfast bar in her very high heels.

'It's fine.' She sighs dramatically. 'I was just leaving. I tried all my best moves, but just he's not falling for it. Are you, Aidan?'

'Not a chance.' He replies, handing her a black folder. 'But thanks all the same.'

'I never quit, Mr Wilder. Just remember that...' Batting her long eyelashes at him, Frankie floats out of the room with a flourish.

'Sorry about that.' Aidan says hurriedly. 'It's a good job you arrived when you did. She would have eaten me alive.'

Not knowing what I want to say, the silence becomes unbearable as Aidan tries to clear the breakfast bar of tools and random catalogues.

'How have you been?' He asks, signalling for me to sit down. 'I've been itching to call you, but with everything that you've had going on I didn't want to bother you. I figured you would call me if you wanted to see me, but then you didn't call and I started to worry. Aldo said...'

His words come to a sudden stop as he turns to look at me.

'Is everything okay, Sadie?'

'I'm fine.' I say quickly, taking a seat at the breakfast bar and avoiding eye contact. 'I'm so sorry for interrupting just now. I shouldn't have come over here without calling first.'

'Don't be silly! I'm so pleased to see you. Frankie, not so much...'

Bringing my eyes up to meet his, I feel a ray of hope.

'Really?'

'Really!' Aidan repeats, sitting down opposite me. 'I was minding my own business and she just stormed in here. All sweetness and light with a field to sell.'

'A field?' I whisper, not quite believing what I am hearing.

'When she showed us around this place, she mentioned that the farmer who owns the land at the bottom of the garden wanted to sell. At the time, I said it was possibly something I would be interested in.' He explains. 'It completely slipped my mind until she waltzed in here with her files and folders.'

'I see...' I reply, not attempting to hide my relief at discovering it was a business meeting I had gatecrashed and not the morning after the night before. 'That explains it.'

'You didn't think something was going on here, did you?'

'Well, you did look rather cosy.'

'Frankie would flirt with a damn tree stump if she thought she was getting a commission.' Laughing loudly, Aidan brushes a pile of sawdust off the bar. 'Like I said, she would have eaten me alive.'

'You don't need to explain yourself to me, Aidan.' Smiling back at him, I feel the tension leave my shoulders. 'It's none of my business who you date and Frankie seems lovely.'

'She's certainly something, but *lovely*, not so much.'

Locking eyes with him, I feel my heart pound as he reaches across the table and places a hand on my arm.

'So, tell me, how have you been?' He asks, with genuine concern. 'I've been thinking about you.'

'I'm doing good now. I just needed some time to come to terms with everything that's happened.' Not being able to take my eyes away from Aidan's hand that is resting on my arm, I try to stop my racing heart. 'It's been a strange couple of weeks.'

Clearly recognising the panicked look on my face, Aidan swiftly removes his hand.

'I'm sorry.' He apologises clumsily. 'I'm just trying to be there for you. Like you were for me.'

'Thank you.' I whisper, wondering why I suddenly feel so awkward around him. 'I appreciate it. I also appreciate you talking to Aldo. You've really helped him to turn a corner.'

'It's no problem. Any friend of yours is a friend of mine.'

The air becomes thick with tension, and something else that I can't quite put my finger on, but it's definitely there, and I know that Aidan feels it, too.

'Where are you up to with the Gavin situation?' He asks. 'Are you going to take a paternity test?'

'I'm still undecided, but I'm trying not think of it right now. I've got bigger fish to fry.'

'Spencer?'

'Not Spencer, but he's something else I need to address. The constant delivery of flowers is starting to become a chore.'

'Flowers?' Aidan repeats, offering me a tiny smile. 'He's still trying to win you over?'

'He's trying to prove that he *could* win me over, which isn't quite the same thing. At first, I was flattered. I was completely blown away that he had come back, but as the days drifted by I started to realise that Spencer doesn't love me. He just loves the idea of me.'

'What about you?' Aidan says quietly. 'What do you want?'

Not daring to look at him, I shrug my shoulders and fiddle with my watch.

'Tell me about these other fish.' Pulling one of the catalogues towards him, Aidan flips through the pages, all the while keeping his eyes on me. 'What else is on your mind?'

Informing Aidan about my mission to change Anxiety Anonymous gives me a rush of adrenaline, in the same way it did when I told Aldo of my plans.

'You constantly amaze me!' He gushes, closing the catalogue. 'Even after all this time, you're still using your anxiety as a catalyst to make a change for the better. You're incredible.'

'I'm just doing what anyone else would do...'

'No, you're not.' Aidan protests. 'Most other people would focus on their own issues and shun everything else. You are amazing, Sadie. You're one in a million.'

He places his hand on my arm once more, only this time it doesn't feel awkward. Some people *are* one in a million. They come along once in a lifetime and make you wonder what you ever did without them, but managing to spot them amongst the rest is what's truly amazing...

Chapter 24

I left the barn soon after that conversation. Being with Aidan makes me feel safe, it makes me feel secure, but it also makes me feel wary. Wary because I don't want to overstep the mark and wary because I don't know why. There's no denying that I feel strongly towards Aidan, but are those feelings of friendship or something more?

Reaching for the photo frame from the bedside table, I open the back and carefully take out the pressed daisy. Moonlight bounces off the petals as I hold the delicate flower in my palm and study it closely. Aidan came into my life in such an unexpected way and left just as unexpectedly. Without any warning, this troubled man appeared before me and I immediately knew he was different from all the rest.

A petal falls from the flower and I watch it slowly float into my lap. It's perfect, but I'm not. Just like everyone else, I'm perfectly imperfect, but Aidan obviously sees something in me I don't. *He came back for you,* the little voice at the back of my mind whispers. *He came back for Cheshire,* I correct, as yet another petal falls from the flower.

Mateo dives onto the bed beside me and I cast my mind back to the day Aidan turned up on the doorstep. I close my eyes and try to recall what it felt like to see him standing there. Only, I don't need to try very hard. Every time I see Aidan I feel the exact same way I did that day. Rolling onto my side, I place the daisy on the pillow and pull the sheets up to my chin. My Unhappiness List winks back at me from its place on the dressing table and I stare back at it with determination. My meeting with Julia has enabled me to make a strong start, but I'm very aware there's still work to do.

Allowing my eyes to close, I find myself drifting into a state of semi-consciousness. You know the kind, those delicious moments when you're not quite asleep, but not really awake either. That period of time, however short, makes nothing else matter. You're in control, yet powerless at the same time. It's really quite beautiful...

Bang! Bang!

Stirring in my sleep, I push myself up onto my elbows and look around the silent bedroom in confusion. Looking equally as perturbed, Mateo lifts his head and *meows* quietly.

Bang! Bang!

I follow the sporadic banging to the window and press my nose against the cold glass. The lane is cast in complete darkness, with the only light coming from the lamp post across the road. Peering into the night, I spot a shadow by the bushes and scowl. Spencer. This is all I need.

Not bothering to grab my dressing gown, I run down the stairs and flick on the light before pulling open the door.

'What the hell are you doing here?' I demand. 'It's the middle of the night!'

Steadying himself on the wall, Spencer swigs from a bottle of beer and gives me a lopsided smile.

'I needed to see you.' He slurs, making no effort to hide how drunk he is. 'I... I needed to talk to you, Sadie.'

Watching him take a seat on the doorstep and hold his head in his hands, I realise this is my chance to put a stop to this once and for all.

'Come in.' I grumble, hardly believing what I'm saying. 'The neighbours will be wondering what's going on.'

I hold open the door and stick out my leg to stop Mateo from darting outside. The four boxes of wilting lilies behind me squeak as I roughly shove them into the corner.

'Well?' I hiss, giving Spencer a nudge with my foot. 'I'm not going to offer again.'

Finally looking up at me with blurry eyes, Spencer holds out a hand to be helped to his feet and stumbles into the cottage. His musky scent is diluted with the smell of stale alcohol and cigarettes, making me grimace as he brushes past me.

Without being invited, he wanders into the living room and drops down onto the couch in an intoxicated heap. Grabbing a cushion, he curls up into a ball and closes his eyes, like a child who has been sleep deprived for weeks on end.

'Don't think you're sleeping there.' I say sternly, perching on the armchair at the opposite side of the room. 'If you've come here for a place to crash for the night, you can think again.'

'Sorry...' Rubbing his red eyes, Spencer blinks repeatedly and shakes his head. 'I'm so sorry.'

Attempting to remain angry, I study Spencer's face and try to find some connection to the man I used to love. His skin is pale and the bags under his eyes are bigger than mine. He certainly doesn't appear to be looking after himself, that's for sure.

'How much have you had to drink?' I ask. 'You look terrible.'

Ignoring my question, Spencer scowls as Mateo pads into the living room.

'What the hell is that?'

'This is Mateo.' I reply haughtily. 'My cat.'

'*You* got a cat?' Spencer says sarcastically, a slight smile playing on his lips. 'You? Seriously?'

'Yes, me! Why is that amusing to you?'

Laughing into his sleeve, he stands up and walks around the living room unsteadily.

'All of this is amusing to me.' He scoffs, gesturing to the beams up ahead. 'What are you trying to prove with all of this?'

'All of what?'

'*This!*' He yells. 'The grandma cottage, the damn cat, the counselling job, the haircut, the whole independent woman act. It's just not you.'

Anger bubbles in the pit of my stomach as Spencer continues to mock my lifestyle choices.

'None of this is you, Sadie. This boring little life isn't yours. Where's the girl I fell in love with? Where's Sadie Valentine?'

Suddenly seeming a lot less drunk than he did five minutes ago, he throws his arms in the air and circles the living room.

'Where's the girl who would get spontaneous tattoos? Where's the girl who ran naked into the sea when she lost a bet? Where's the girl who would spend hours on the beach in the rain, not caring that she was soaked to the bone? Where's the girl who loved to drink tequila in her penthouse apartment? Where's the girl who threw caution to the wind and lived every day as though it was her last?'

Crouching down in front of me, Spencer reaches for my hand and I allow him to take it.

'Stop this.' He continues. 'Let's wipe the slate clean and start again. Let's forget the past and move on. You don't need to keep pretending to be this person.'

Considering my response for a moment before I answer, I smile at my finger tattoo and feel a sense of calm wash over me.

'Do you want to know what happened to that girl, Spencer? To the crazy young girl you knew? To the girl who loved without reservation? To the girl who had never been hurt and believed the future was going to be bright and full of happiness?'

Waiting to assess his reaction, I stare into the eyes that used to make me so deliriously happy.

'She grew up, Spencer, and you made that happen. You made her realise that life isn't a bed of roses and that heartbreak can happen to you when you least expect it. She became hardened to the outside world and learnt to develop a thick skin. The way you treated her left her broken, but she managed to piece herself together again. She may appear to be fixed, but she'll never be the same person she was before. The cracks will always be there, if you look hard enough.'

Finally taking my hand out of his, I smile sadly and brush his hair out of his face.

'The girl you knew is gone, but I should be thanking you for that. I really should. If I wouldn't have met you, I would never have become the person I was always meant to be. I would still be self-absorbed, materialistic and with no idea of which direction my life was going in. Thanks to you, I have learnt how to be truly happy. It just so happens that the happiness came from losing you, not being with you. My *boring life,* as you put it, means more to me than you could ever understand. Blossom View, Anxiety Anonymous, Mateo... This is who I am now, and I couldn't be prouder to say that.'

Blinking repeatedly, he screws up his nose and rubs his face agitatedly.

'What are you talking about? Of course, you're still you. Just... just stop with the riddles and say that we can start again.' Taking my hand once more, he points to my tattoo. '*Forever*. See? What more proof do you need that we're meant to be together? We were there once and we can get there again.'

'You don't want me, Spencer. The girl who you're looking for doesn't exist anymore, and the woman I am now is as far away from her as could possibly be.' I say firmly, standing to my feet. 'You promised me that if I told you to stop trying, you would walk away and never look back. This is me telling you to stop. Please stay true to your word and leave. There's nothing for you here.'

Staring at me in silence, Spencer frowns sceptically, expecting me to laugh and say that of course, I would take him back. His dark eyes narrow as he studies my unflinching face for a glimmer of doubt in what I am saying, but he won't find one. There's no longer a single part of me that is longing for him. He is part of my past and his treatment of me has helped to shape my future, but he isn't part of it.

'Please leave now.' I persist, motioning to the door. 'Go back to Brighton and move on with your life.'

'It doesn't have to be like this, Sadie.'

'You're right.' I reply, holding Mateo against my chest. 'We don't have to part ways like this. You don't have to leave under a cloud, but you do have to leave. So, you have two choices. You can walk out of that door and never bother me again, or we can shake hands, for old times' sake, and wish each other luck for the future.'

Holding out my spare hand, my heart races as he stares at me before finally accepting it.

'Goodbye, Spencer.' My voice is calm and steady as I shake his hand firmly. 'Take care.'

Without saying a word, he walks out of the living room and pauses by the front door. With his hand on the doorknob, he looks over his shoulder before stepping outside into the darkness.

To get closure, you have to shut the door and move on. Although, it's not closing the door that's the hard part, it's having confidence in yourself to *finally* throw away the key...

Chapter 25

'Despite the name above the door offering anonymity to anyone who enters this room, none of you come here to be anonymous. You come here to be part of a group who understand what it is you're going through. Uniting as one is what we do here on a daily basis. It's what we have always done and what we will continue to do in the future.'

The Anxiety Anonymous meeting is due to end very shortly, which leaves me just ten minutes to let the support group in on my plans to change the name of the charity.

'First impressions count for everything and I'd like to think that here at Anxiety Anonymous, we always make a good one, but first impressions are often established before people even step over the threshold. We all judge books by their covers, even if we don't mean to, so it's only natural that some people will fall at the first hurdle when they consider coming along to a meeting.'

A confused murmur flits around the group as they try to work out where I am going with this.

'The word *anonymous* means unacknowledged, nameless and incognito. None of those words do I believe should be associated with mental health. And more importantly, none of those words accurately describe what we do here. The reality is that we battle anxiety together. The word *together* means side by side, hand in hand, and shoulder to shoulder. It means in unison, it means with each other, and it means as one...'

My skin tingles as I gear myself up for the big moment. If the guys here are against the name change, it's a likely indicator that the board of directors will be, too.

'With that in mind, I have proposed that the name of the charity be changed...'

'Change the name of the charity?' Alec interrupts, frowning in confusion. 'Why? What to?'

Holding my breath, I cross my fingers beneath the folder on my lap.

'I spoke with Julia yesterday and she is supporting me in my mission to change Anxiety Anonymous to... Anxiety Together.'

'Anxiety Together?' Repeating the name to himself, Alec loosens his tie and nods appreciatively. 'I like it. Anxiety Together! What a great idea!'

'I'm so glad you think so...' I reply, breathing a sigh of relief. 'Because this is my first, and probably last, chance to make this happen, but I can't do it alone...'

'Then it's a good job you don't have to.' Turning his chair around to face the rest of the circle, Alec address the room. 'Isn't that right, guys?'

A chorus of excited chatter come back at him as I look around the group.

'I think it's a great idea...'

'Count me in...'

'It sounds so much more welcoming...'

My heart swells with pride as I listen to their words of encouragement. Getting the vote of confidence from the support group is another step towards making this happen.

'You have no idea how much your backing of this means to me. The power in removing the taboo surrounding mental health lies in numbers...'

As I tell the support group the many ways in which they can help me in my mission, I marvel at how easy it has been to get them on board. It seems that any slight opportunity to make a stand for mental health sufferers is welcomed with open arms. Within five minutes of mentioning my plans, I have Alec starting a petition, Yvette offering a written statement of support, and other members gushing over what a fabulous idea this is.

'When is the meeting with the board of directors?' Alec asks, taking a notepad from his briefcase.

'Wednesday.' I reply, delighted they are taking so much interest.

'So, just two days?'

Nodding back at him, I glance at the calendar on my desk.

'I know it's not long to prepare, but this is the only slot Julia could secure for the next six months.'

'Ahh...' Alec mumbles uncertainly, looking deep in thought. 'What time?'

'Midday.'

'So, the time we would normally meet here?'

'Yes...'

Falling into silence, Alec taps a pen against his notepad before standing up and addressing the rest of the attendees.

'I've got an idea.' He says authoritatively. 'Sadie said the power is in numbers, right? Then what better way to bring this to the board of directors than by doing it together?'

'But how?' Yvette replies, scribbling her name down on Alec's makeshift petition and passing it along. 'There's around thirty of us here, how could we all attend the meeting?'

Marching over to the whiteboard, Alec points to the projector at the back of the room.

'At work, we have meetings with our clients in Chicago via video link. What's to stop us gathering here as usual and putting our thoughts to the directors? We'd be here anyway and I'm sure we would all love to have our voices heard?'

As the rest of the room indicate they are keen to be involved, Alec fist-pumps the air.

'We're forming an anxiety army!' He chants, to the joyful cheers of the others.

Hearing the door squeak open, I look to my left and feel my smile drop slightly when my mum walks into the meeting. Without making eye contact, she slips behind the circle of chairs and perches on the coffee table at the back of the room. We haven't seen one another since the fundraiser and as a result, my stomach is doing somersaults. Admittedly, I've ignored her calls and steady stream of text messages, but that's only because I don't have a clue what to say to her...

'Sadie?' Alec says, reaching over and tapping my arm. 'What do you think?'

Tearing my eyes away from my mum, I clear my throat and nod in agreement.

'I think it's an amazing idea. Like you said, what better way to bring this to the board of directors than by doing it together?'

'Exactly!' Alec cheers, clearly enjoying his role as leader of the group. 'All for one and one for all...'

*   *   *

'So...' My mum begins, stirring a straw around her glass slowly. 'This is... erm... yeah...'

Smiling back at her, I stare into the bottom of my own drink and keep pretending that everything is perfectly fine. The fact that she's ordered a double vodka is enough to make me worry about what she's going to say next, although, if her strained attempts at conversation are anything to go by, it's going to be a while before she gathers the courage to spit it out.

'They have some lovely dishes here, don't they?' She muses, feigning interest. 'The tapas menu sounds delicious. Have you been here before?'

I nod back at her and focus on tearing my napkin into tiny pieces.

'The lampshades are quirky, aren't they?' Straining her neck, she points to the funky light fittings and fakes a captivated smile. 'They remind me of...'

'What do you really want to talk about, Mum?' I ask, finally tiring of the small talk. 'Because I'm guessing you didn't gatecrash my support group to talk about the light fittings.'

Her face pales as she stares back at me in an emotional silence.

'I've been calling you.' She mumbles, copying my actions and ripping her napkin in two.

'I know, I've not been too well.' I lie. 'You know how it is when your stomach isn't quite right.'

A knowing smile creeps onto her lips and I can't help but return it.

'Like mother, like daughter.' She says gently. 'These upset stomachs must run in the family.'

Replying with nothing more than a simple shrug of the shoulders, I wait for her to tell me what this impromptu meeting is about.

'Your idea for the charity sounds good. *Anxiety Together* has a much better ring to it. Did you see me signing the petition at the meeting?'

'Well, it's about a bit more than it just sounding better.' I explain, almost curtly. 'The message is so much more significant than that.'

'No, I mean, yes, of course, it's more significant than that, but...'

'It's fine.' I reply, really hoping to move the conversation along. 'But thank you for signing the petition. I appreciate it.'

We fall into silence once more and I suddenly become rather agitated. We both know why we're here and we both know how awkward it is going to be to talk about it.

'Gavin Gastrell.' I say abruptly, resting my hands on the table. 'There, I've said it.'

Reaching for her glass, she throws back the contents in one and wipes her mouth on the torn napkin.

'Listen, Sadie, I have a few things I need to say to you.' Keeping her gaze fixed on mine, she folds her arms defensively. 'First of all, I am sorry for not addressing the subject of your father with you sooner.

You have every right to know who he is and I should have respected that a long time ago. Secondly, I was telling you the truth when I said I don't know who he is, but if you wish to try and find him, I will help you in any way that I can...'

My heart races as I listen to her speak, not daring to breathe a word in case I stop her flow.

'I know it will be hard. It will be almost impossible.' She continues. 'But I'll do whatever it takes to get you the answers you need. It's the least you deserve. And finally, I am terribly sorry for running away from this situation and putting my own feelings before yours...'

A rowdy group enters the bar behind us, but the only thing I can hear is my mum's voice.

'I feel like we have made great progress in fixing our relationship and I don't want to undo our hard work. We had come so far before all this. I was really enjoying the time we were spending together. It made me realise just how consumed with... *myself* I have been.'

With Mick. I correct, reading between the lines of what she is saying. Mick has always been the divider between my mum and I. It doesn't take a genius to work out that he isn't going to be happy about this. Mick will cause a riot if he finds out my mum is going in search of a man she has been intimate with. His jealous streak will make this a *lot* more difficult than it needs to be.

'What about Mick?' I whisper, almost not believing we are having this conversation.

'I'll deal with Mick.' She replies firmly. 'Just leave Mick to me.'

Taking this as an end to the conversation, I reach across the table and take her hand in mine. It might have taken us a little while to get here, but there's no denying we have come along leaps and bounds.

As she smiles back at me, clearly relieved to have said what she wanted to say, I debate telling her about the DNA test. She's adamant that Gavin isn't my father, but something is telling me that she's wrong. Call it a hunch, a hope or a misguided belief, but there's something in his eyes that makes me think otherwise.

'Mum, about Gavin...'

'Sadie, you don't need to concern yourself with Gavin.' Shaking her head, she squeezes my hand tightly. 'He is not your man. You have to trust me on this.'

I hesitantly nod back at her and decide to keep the paternity test to myself. She doesn't need to know my opinion and I don't need to tell her. Besides, if she's right, there won't be anything to tell...

Chapter 26

Perching on the windowsill, I watch the postman as he quietly moves from house to house and wonder how many times I have sat in this very spot lately. Sitting here and watching the world go by while I think about things has become a normal part of my daily routine. I should be in the kitchen enjoying my breakfast right now, but I can't face anything. I have dreaded this moment all night. The torment of not knowing how to handle Gavin's last day here kept me awake well into the early hours and I'm still undecided now.

I thought it would be a relief to say goodbye to Jason and his team. To wave off the rubble, the disruption and the general chaos of having a group of burly men in the house. Only, the chaos isn't the only thing I'm saying adios to, is it? Just a few short weeks ago, I was so excited to welcome my shiny kitchen and dining room to the cottage, but the truth is, I haven't really given my gleaming new interior a second thought. Until now, anyway.

You see, once I shake hands with Jason, pay him his money and thank him for his work, that's it. The window of opportunity with Gavin will be closed. I can't see me ever reaching out to him in the future as I firmly believe this was our chance. The stars aligned to make our paths cross at this very point, despite my mother's insistence otherwise.

After hiding from him since he gave me the paternity test, I feel incredibly nervous about seeing Gavin, but deep down, I know that I have to. Although I haven't decided what I am going to say, I simply cannot let him leave without seeing him one last time. Knowing I am potentially his daughter must be weighing heavily on his mind. After all, I'm not the only one affected by this. Gavin's life could be turned upside down at the opening of an envelope, but he took the risk anyway. To him, it seemed worth it.

The test is still safely tucked away in the zipped compartment of my handbag. I haven't looked at it for days, but every second that passes I am aware that it's there. The idea of a simple cheek swab changing my life is terrifying. Not because of what it might tell me, but because of what it won't. If Gavin isn't my father, where does that leave me? My mum's offer to help me find my biological dad gives me hope, but I'm not convinced it's something I want to pursue. Right now, the lid is on the tin, but it has been opened just enough to grab my curiosity and get me thinking, *what if?*

Spotting Jason's tired van racing along the lane, I give myself a pep talk before walking down the hallway to greet him.

'The wanderer returns!' Jason trills, beaming brightly as I open the door.

'Hi, Jason.' Moving aside, I smile as he steps inside the cottage. 'Sorry I haven't been here. Things have been rather hectic lately.'

'I know that feeling all too well, love. We're starting a renovation project in Oldham tomorrow. Stripping it back to the bare bones. The whole lot is coming out...'

Heading into the kitchen as another builder follows his lead, Jason continues to shout over his shoulder. 'We shouldn't be long today, Sadie. Couple of hours and we'll be out of your hair. The grouting on these tiles will need a day or so to fully set...'

I hear Jason's words, but I can't process them as my eyes are fixed on the deserted van by the side of the road. Gavin's not here. He hasn't turned up. They say you don't know what you're wishing for until the option is taken away from you, and it would appear that I've learnt that the hard way. I had so many opportunities. So many days to take the damn test, but I didn't. I brushed it under the carpet and tried to pretend it wasn't happening. I buried my head in the sand, refusing to acknowledge it until it was too late and now I've missed my chance. The door has shut, the gate has closed, the...

Hearing a bang, I turn around to see another pair of feet jumping out of the van.

'Gavin!' I exclaim, a sense of relief hitting my stomach. 'You came!'

Trying to disguise his terrified expression behind a forced smile, Gavin takes a toolbox from the back of the van and slowly makes his way along the garden path.

'I had no choice, love! Jason doesn't drop the whip until we've signed off on a job. He'd have had my guts for garters if I pulled another sickie!'

I laugh along nervously, not daring to look directly at him in case he disappears.

'Do you have a moment to talk?' I ask quietly, allowing the door to close behind me.

'Of course.' Nodding enthusiastically, he places the toolbox on the doorstep. 'Come to the van. I don't want those two earwigging.'

Without saying a word, I follow him to the van and give the dirty seat a dubious glance before pulling open the door.

'Sorry about the mess.' Frantically trying to clear the passenger seat, Gavin knocks a collection of empty cigarette packets and mouldy sandwich wrappers onto the floor. 'That's Jason, that is. He's a right pig. Treats this van like it's a tip. You'd think squatters had been in here...'

'It's fine! Honestly.' Avoiding a pair of pliers, I hop onto the seat and close the door with a bang.

Empty coffee cups roll around beneath my trainers as I attempt to place my feet out of harm's way.

'The fundraiser was good.' Gavin says uneasily, wiping a layer of dust off the dashboard. 'Your speech really got me going. Makes you think, doesn't it?'

I mumble in agreement and resist the urge to clear away the mess.

'It's hard to believe you've had a hard time upstairs, love. You're too pretty to have something like that...' His face falls as he quickly tries to correct what he's just said. 'That came out all wrong. I'm always putting my bloody foot in it. What I mean is, a beautiful young girl like yourself shouldn't have to deal with something like that. It's not right. It's not fair.'

'Thank you.' I reply, very aware that he's beating himself up inside. 'One of our main goals at the charity is to change people's perception about mental health. Anxiety and depression can affect anyone.

They don't care who you are or what you have. They really aren't picky.'

'I'm sorry you've had to experience that, love.' A sad expression creeps onto Gavin's face and he wipes his right eye with his sleeve. 'You don't deserve that.'

'Well, nobody does, but with one in four people being affecting by mental health problems, the odds aren't exactly favourable.' Stealing a glance at him, I notice him wiping his eyes once more and try to move the conversation along. 'Did your family have a good time at the fundraiser?'

'Oh, they absolutely loved it.' He gushes. 'She's still banging on about it now is our Angela. Complaining that we can't move down here ourselves. She'd bleed me dry if I let her.'

I smile back at him, very aware of the humongous elephant that's in here with us.

'So, did you... did you take the test?' Gavin asks quietly, his voice barely audible over the noise of a passing tractor. 'Why am I even asking? Of course, you have taken the test. That's why you're here.'

Staring back at him, I shake my head slowly. There's no need to drag this out. There's no point beating around the bush. I just need to tell him my decision.

'I'm not taking the test, but I need you to know why...' Licking my dry lips, I try to get my words out without becoming emotional. 'The fact that you were willing to do this means so much to me. It really is an incredible testament to your character and I will be forever grateful.'

A flicker of hurt hits Gavin's eyes and he stares down at his lap.

'I've thought about this long and hard, but I can't bring myself to open this can of worms. My mum is adamant that you're not my father and if she's right, taking that test will leave a huge question mark over who is.'

'I respect your decision, love.' He replies, a sad tone to his voice. 'You don't have to do anything you don't want to do.'

I open my mouth to respond, but he beats me to it.

'We were just a pair of teenagers from the wrong side of the tracks. Your mum, she had a reputation, and I'm not saying that to be spiteful, it's just the way she was. She told me she was pregnant pretty early on and claimed she didn't know who the father was. We went our separate ways and the rest is history. I'm not proud of not sticking around to find out, far from it. I should have found her before now. I should have tracked her down and insisted she take a test. I'll never forgive myself for not doing that. I won't.'

'You don't need to beat yourself up.' I whisper. 'We've all made mistakes. It's what makes us human.'

'I just want you to know that I'm sorry, Sadie. I need you *and* your mum to both know that. I respect your decision, I really do, but if you take the test and it turns out I am your father...'

'If she was telling me differently, I would take the test right now. I just don't want to be left with a hole that wasn't really there before.' I say gently, hoping he understands. 'When I was younger, I often wondered who my dad was. I even went to find you once before...'

Snapping his head up, Gavin frowns as he waits for me to explain.

'When?' He asks, looking understandably floored. 'How?'

'When I was a teenager, I asked about my dad and my mum gave me your name on a piece of paper. Last year, I looked you up online and drove to your address. I thought I would immediately know, you know? But I didn't. I watched you from the side of the road, but I didn't feel anything at all. We even exchanged a few words, but I felt nothing.'

Seemingly stunned into silence, Gavin clears his throat and rubs his brow.

'I have to disagree with you, love. I could see it as soon as Linda walked into that cottage and I have seen it every day since. I can see your eyes in Paige's when I'm at home. I can see your smile in Mitch's. It has to be me, Sadie. I'm your dad. I just know it.'

A tear slips down my cheek and I quickly wipe it away.

'I thought I could see it too, but is that because we want it to be true, or because that bond really is there?'

Shrugging his shoulders, Gavin rubs his face and turns to look out of the window. He wants to be my dad. No one has ever wanted to fill that role in my life. No one has ever thought me worthy enough to risk losing everything for.

Before I can stop it, a sob escapes my lips and I cover my mouth to hide it.

'Don't cry, love.' Wrapping an arm around my shoulders, Gavin pulls me towards him and I silently cry into his chest. 'Please don't cry.'

He smells of coffee and fresh paint, but it's comforting in a way I can't quite describe. His t-shirt quickly becomes saturated with my tears as I hold on to him like a little girl who has lost her parents in a shopping centre. Scared, frightened, and just needing to be reassured that everything will be okay.

Finally composing myself, I wipe my damp face and smile sadly when I realise his eyes are also glassy.

'What must we look like?' I say between sniffles. 'Crying in a van like this before most people have even had their morning coffee.'

Laughing lightly, Gavin hands me a crumpled tissue from his pocket and rubs his own eyes with his sleeve.

'Don't worry. It is clean. It's just been screwed up in my pocket, that's all.'

Gratefully accepting it, I remove what is left of my mascara before speaking once more.

'If I take that test, one way or another my life will change forever, and right now I am happy with my life as it is.' His face falls once more and I swallow the lump in my throat. 'Please don't think my decision is any reflection on you, Gavin, because it isn't. I can only hope that you understand.'

'Of course, I understand.' He replies quickly, not missing a beat. 'If you are okay with not knowing, I will respect that. It's the least I can do for you, but if you ever change your mind, you know where to find me.'

Not daring to speak unless I erupt into tears once more, I offer him a tiny nod in response and reach for the door handle.

'And that goes for everything...' He adds. 'Everything and anything. If you ever want a shoulder to cry on, money, advice, or a tubby kitchen fitter to redo Jason's tiles that will inevitably fall off once your warranty expires...'

Despite feeling so sad, I laugh as Gavin's green eyes crinkle into his smile.

'Like I said, you know where to find me.'

Smiling back at him, I give him a final nod before jumping out of the van. Resisting the urge to look back, I walk straight to my car and jump into the driver's seat. Quickly turning on the engine, I pull away from the kerb and keep my eyes fixed on the road ahead.

It's a funny thing, closure, isn't it? We all seek it in one form or the other. To move on, to shut one door before opening another, but what if deciding not to take the test *is* my closure? Who's to argue that this isn't what I've been searching for to draw a line beneath it and move on? After all, *I* am the one making the decision not to take the test. *I* am the one in control of what happens next.

As hard as I'm trying to convince myself of this theory, the little voice in the back of my mind tells me that some chapters of our lives aren't meant to have closure. It whispers that some stories are destined to be left unfinished, incomplete and without a conclusion, because some things are *never* meant to end...

Chapter 27

My talk with Gavin earlier got me thinking about stories. From fairy tales and mysteries to comedies and tragedies, they all have the same three things in common. A beginning, a middle and an end. We all carry our own stories with us through life, whether they be good or bad, and I am no exception. We keep them close to our hearts and try to see them through to the end, even when we're not sure if we're going to like where they take us. With this in mind, I came to the place where all the greatest stories call home. I came to the library.

I didn't want to be with Aidan, Aldo, my mum, or even Mateo. I just wanted to be alone. Alone with my thoughts and alone with myself. I had an urge to escape my own story and lose myself in the stories of others. Looking at the many rows of books around me, I study the beautiful covers and feel a sense of warmth wash over me. Thousands of titles clutter the shelves, each one dogeared and covered in laminated plastic. They say you shouldn't judge a book by its cover, but to me, all covers are the same. They simply protect what's inside like a shield, keeping their precious pages safe from the rest of the world until they're plucked from the shelf and devoured by an avid reader.

Thinking about my own life, I wonder how many people would enjoy my story so far. It's certainly been a roller coaster ride, that's for sure. There have been more ups and downs than I thought I could handle, but I have ridden the waves and exited in one piece. Yes, I have the battle wounds, but I'm still here and I'm ready to acquire some more.

The stash of papers on the table in front of me catches my attention and I get back to the task at hand. I didn't just come to the library to escape into another world, I came here to get inspiration for where my own might take me. The presentation to the board of directors at the charity takes place in just forty-eight hours, which doesn't leave me much time to tie up any loose ends. Having the backing of my nearest and dearest, the support group and Julia, this should be a walk in the park, but knowing I have just one shot at this is making me question myself.

Do I know exactly what it is I want to say? Are the facts and figures I have been rehearsing definitely correct? Did I get permission from the Anxiety Anonymous members to use their statements?

The truth is, I know the answer to all of those questions, but how much can you really rehearse for something? How much is from memory and how much is from the heart?

Running my fingers across the many printouts and handwritten declarations, I feel a surge of adrenaline. My entire journey over the past twelve months has been leading to this moment. To the opportunity to make a real change. A change that will benefit so many people for years to come. It makes it all worthwhile. Every day is a new opportunity to offer help and advice to people who are feeling as terrible as

I once did, and now I have a chance to help remove the stigma around mental health. Me. Little old Sadie Valentine. Silly Shirley who had a breakdown is now preparing for the biggest presentation of her life.

It's funny how life works, isn't it? I've never been particularly religious, but if God, the universe, or fate has a plan for me, they have pulled off something pretty spectacular. Just a year ago, I was drinking bubbles and wearing inappropriate dresses while desperately trying to fit in with the wrong company. Now, I am spending my time organising statements and filing petitions in a bid to change the name of one of the biggest mental health charities in the United Kingdom.

Picking up my pen, I get comfortable in my seat and start numbering the points I wish to highlight. We all want to put our stamp on the world before we leave, and I have been given the perfect chance to do exactly that. Not in a way that is life-changing to most people, but in a way that could bring a ray of hope to a few...

Chapter 28

Most people feel blessed if they can say they have a best friend, yet I am lucky enough to have two. Aidan might not have been in my life for very long, but I already know that he isn't going anywhere. How? Well, I don't really know how. Sometimes, a person stumbles into your life and you wonder what you ever did without them. Just like the day I met Aldo. I knew from the very moment Aldo and I first spoke that he would be in my life forever. What I didn't know was just how much he would mean to me. He's more than my friend, he's my other half. Not in a romantic way, obviously, but in a way that means we have a bond that simply can't be broken.

Looking on as Aldo and Aidan chat animatedly with one another, I lean back in my seat and smile to myself. I haven't spoken to Aldo about my growing feelings for Aidan and I don't think I need to. I'm pretty sure Aldo has clocked the way my cheeks blush when Aidan looks at me. He makes my stomach feel like it's being attacked by a flurry of butterflies in a way that is impossible to hide. No matter how hard I try to convince myself otherwise, he makes me smile like I haven't smiled before...

'To Shirley!' Aldo says, nudging my arm and holding his glass in the air.

'I haven't given the presentation yet.' I protest. 'Don't you think this is a little presumptuous?'

'This isn't about the presentation.' Aldo shuffles around the booth and throws a leather-clad arm around my shoulder. 'Whatever happens tomorrow, it won't change the fact that you are absolutely amazing.'

'I second that.' Aidan adds, smiling at me from across the table. 'Sadie the Great!'

Brushing off their compliments, I clink my glass against theirs and take a tiny sip. The funny thing is, I *am* feeling pretty bloody great right now. The stars are aligning and everything is falling into its natural place. Aidan is back, Aldo has recovered from Edward, Spencer has finally crawled back under his rock, I have made peace with not knowing who my father is, and my career is taking me to places I never dreamed of. Aldo's right. Regardless of the outcome of the presentation, the future is looking rather bright indeed.

'So, what's next for you?' Aldo asks Aidan, who is leisurely flicking through the local newspaper. 'What does life have in store for Aidan Wilder?'

'I honestly don't know and for the first time in my life, I am completely okay with that.' He replies breezily, closing the paper. 'All I am certain of is that my future lies right here. Apart from that, who knows? But wherever it takes me and whatever it brings, I know that I am ready...'

Listening to Aidan speak, I feel my heart swell with pride. Anxiety has taken so much away from me, but it has also brought me so much. So many friends, so much hope and so much drive. That's the funny thing with anxiety. It opens your eyes to what you couldn't see before. It makes you aware that everyone is fighting a battle that you probably know nothing about. It makes you compassionate to others and grateful for the times where anxiety isn't holding you back. It makes you realise you are stronger than you think and braver than you believe.

They say that every cloud has a silver lining and I couldn't relate to that more if I tried. Anxiety changed my life forever, in ways I never dreamed possible. Will tomorrow's meeting take me down yet another path I didn't see coming, or will I still be here? Still happy, still content and still looking forward to what the future holds? Either way, I can't wait to find out...

* * *

Staring up at the ceiling, I rub my face and let out a frustrated sigh. The clock by the side of the bed reminds me that it's the middle of the night. Teasing me with its red numbers as the minutes turn into hours. The more I panic about not achieving the full eight hours of sleep I require, the further I drift from it. My eyes are wide open and my legs are refusing to keep still.

I have to be awake in just four hours, yet I simply cannot drift off. My body is buzzing with adrenaline and my mind is alive with arguments I want to make in favour of the charity name change. I know exactly what I want to say and when I need to say it, but my brain simply will not settle down.

Stretching out on the soft sheets, I spot Mateo snoring at the foot of the bed and feel a pang of envy. With his tail curled around him and his nose buried into his paws, he looks so calm and serene. As I look on, he purrs gently in his sleep, like a fluffy cloud that is getting ready to effortlessly float into the atmosphere.

Mimicking his actions, I pull my legs up to my chin and squeeze my eyes tightly shut.

...One in four people will be affected by mental health issues...
...If we want to remove the stigma from anxiety, we have to go back to basics...
...Speaking as someone who has experienced anxiety first-hand, I can testify that the whole ethos of being anonymous...

Kicking my legs in defeat, I throw back the covers and walk around the bed in my pyjamas. Everything seems eerily quiet and still, reminding me that I should be sleeping right now like the rest of Cheshire. Pausing by my dressing table, I wipe a thin layer of dust from the mirror and frown when I notice a chip in my otherwise perfect manicure. Once I notice it, I can't see anything else. Deciding to pass some time by fixing the offending nail, I pull out the chair and curse when my handbag falls to the floor with a thud.

Reaching down to retrieve it, I groan when the contents spill out across the carpet. Hurriedly stuffing my lipstick, a book of stamps and a tin of Vaseline back into the handbag, I curse myself for not staying in bed. I should have just had a glass of brandy and whacked a relaxing tape on. I should have tried counting sheep. I should have...

My hand freezes as it lands on an envelope at the bottom of my handbag. Slowly pulling it out from beneath my collection of lip balms, I flick on the lamp and hold the envelope in my hands. The test. The test that I had decided I didn't want to do. Peeling it open, I calmly take out the printed sheet of paper and read over the text. For the first time since Gavin gave it to me, I read it and I read it properly. I read every line and every word twice over. The instructions are simple enough. A quick cheek swab popped into a prepaid envelope. That's all there is to it. Taking the two test tubes, I place Gavin's on the dressing table and hold the other in my hand.

Without giving it another thought, I walk into the bathroom and position myself in front of the mirror. My fingers slowly release the cap and take out the wand as I stare at my reflection in complete silence. Twirling the swab between my fingers, I raise it to my lips and slowly open my mouth. The bristles feel rough as I rub the wand against my cheek, making sure to coat both sides before slipping it back into the bottle and fastening the cap.

Heading back into the bedroom, I fill in the label and place both bottles into the designated envelope before sealing it. Only minutes have passed since I crept out of bed, but the room feels lighter and less suffocating than it did just moments ago. Allowing myself a few deep breaths to appreciate the sense of relief that is washing over me, I turn off the lamp before slipping under the sheets once more.

The second my head hits the pillow I feel my body melt into the mattress and this time I don't fight it. Whatever was keeping me awake has vanished and in its place is an overwhelming desire to sleep. A desire so strong, it completely overrides my ability to do anything else. Legend says, when you can't sleep at night, it's because you're awake in someone else's dream and as my eyes finally close, I can't help but wonder whose?

Chapter 29

The boardroom is much bigger than I imagined it would be and apart from an enormous table, it's completely empty. Said table is surrounded by at least twenty solemn business people. All wearing slick suits and sharp glasses, their intense stares are making me even more nervous than I was before. Trying to appear cool, calm and collected, I nod back at them and focus on placing my prompt cards on the chair in front of me.

Julia is sitting at the back of the room, along with a young girl from HR, who is taking notes on a tiny laptop. Seemingly unfazed by the scary set-up, Julia flashes me the thumbs-up sign and grins like a proud mother. Giving her a brief nod in response, I fiddle with the remote control for the PowerPoint presentation and silently recite my speech in my mind.

The entire support group is waiting at the Anxiety Anonymous meeting room, fully prepared and ready to offer their input. I haven't told Julia about the video link. As far as she is aware, my laptop is positioned in front of the projector screen to display my speech notes and nothing more. Keeping this to myself might seem fruitless, but it's my trump card. It's my crowning glory. My big finish. If my speech alone doesn't win them over, then the guys at the support group are my last hope...

'We're ready for you.' An extremely tall lady says authoritatively. 'The next meeting starts in twenty minutes, so I suggest you use your time wisely.'

Retreating to a seat at the head of the table, she clicks her pen repeatedly, indicating that it's time for me to get moving. Not wanting to waste a moment, I give my prompt cards one last glance before speaking.

'My name is Sadie Valentine.' I begin, silently cursing myself for forgetting to say hello. 'Some of you may know me as a counsellor for the Wilmslow branch of Anxiety Anonymous and others won't know me at all, but regardless of being already acquainted, what you all probably don't know is... I am an anxiety sufferer. Like Julia, I was introduced to the charity at a very low point in my life. I watched the bubbly girl everyone knew and loved crumble into a sad, lonely and frightened woman. I was afraid, more afraid than I have ever been in my entire life, but Anxiety Anonymous helped change that.'

Clasping my hands together in front of me, I take a step forward and smile warmly.

'Before my experience with anxiety, I didn't put much thought into the subject of mental health. The truth is, if it isn't happening to you or those around you, we have a tendency to cast it aside and carry on with our own lives regardless. But once you are hit with it, and one in four people *will* be affected by mental health issues, you start to realise just how many obstacles there are facing sufferers...'

A man with a clipboard raises his hand in the air, bringing my speech to a swift stop.

'It really isn't necessary to prep us on the stats of mental health. We're all up to date on the figures...'

A laugh titters around the room and I feel my cheeks burn with embarrassment.

'Continue with your presentation, but skip past any facts and figures as we simply don't have the time.' Pushing his clipboard away, he positions his glasses on the bridge of his nose. 'Please, continue.'

'What... what I would...' Completely flummoxed by the unexpected and rather abrupt interruption, I struggle to find my flow. 'The name of the charity signifies...'

My heart pounds in my chest as I realise I am losing them already.

'Okay, you want me to get straight to it? Here it is. *Anonymous*. It screams everything that mental health should *not* be associated with. The concept of something being anonymous generates the idea that anxiety is something we should be embarrassed of and therefore have to address secretly. I am here to tell you that ideology is as far away from the reality as it could possibly be. It's the twenty-first century and yet we *still* haven't removed the stigma surrounding mental health. Unfortunately, it is still a subject we shy away from. Despite many advances in the world of mental health, people just aren't as comfortable talking about it in the way they would any other bodily ailment. And that is where you guys come into play...'

Looking at the clock on the wall behind Julia, I realise my time is running out and I still haven't made half of the points I wish to make.

'As one of the largest mental health charities in the United Kingdom, you have an incredible amount of influence over the general public. Being someone who deals with members of the public on a daily basis, I can tell you that Anxiety Anonymous is giving out the wrong message entirely.'

A flash of annoyance hits the clipboard guy's eyes, but I continue regardless.

'I work with people who cower at the back of the support group, too afraid to mumble their own name in case they are identified and ridiculed for being there. As someone who did the exact same thing when I walked through those doors for the first time, I asked myself *why?* Why do people feel the need to distance themselves from their mental health? And the answer is because of things exactly like this - Anxiety Anonymous. If we want to change the opinion of mental health, we have to strip back everything we know and start again. We have to erase what we think and rewrite the rules. Nobody should feel the need to attend an anonymous support group to get help for their mental health. We have to come together. We *need* to come together. We need to create a welcome, caring and open environment for people to flock to. Not the kind of place sufferers attend under the cover of darkness, using a fake name and a disguise, but somewhere they can feel part of a community.'

Finally stopping for breath, I reach for the remote to the projector and hold it behind my back.

'I am proud to say that in Wilmslow, we *have* that community. The relaxed, honest and casual approach we have taken in our meetings has had a profound effect on those in attendance. How have we achieved that? By coming together as one. As one friendship circle, as one family, as one entity. And who better to tell you more about that, than the members of the support group themselves...'

A few surprised looks come back at me as a confused murmur buzzes around the room. Not being deterred, I hit play and step to the side as the projector springs into life.

Here goes. It's all or nothing...

After a brief delay, Alec appears on the screen and positions himself in front of the webcam.

'Hello, my name is Alec Anderson and I have been attending Anxiety Anonymous meetings here for probably longer then what is necessary. Why? I hear you ask. Why would someone want to attend a support group for a second longer than they have to? Well, the answer is very simple. Friends. Friends are what I call all of these people here...'

Alec holds the webcam higher to reveal row after row of smiling faces behind him.

'When I first came here, I was mortified that people might find out. The idea that anyone might know I was struggling upstairs was almost worse than the anxiety itself, but all that has changed for me now. These days, I come here when anxiety gets the best of me, but I also come when I am feeling okay and the reason for that is to help others...'

As Alec continues to talk, I look over my shoulder and smile when I see Julia staring open-mouthed.

'This is a support group like no other. We have a circle of chairs and a counsellor who oversees our meetings, but that is where the similarities to other meetings stop. Of course, people are scared at first, but that fear gradually subsides. After a while, people come here because there's a sense of togetherness. There's a feeling that once you step through the door, you are no longer alone in your troubles and that is where the word *anonymous* is so ill-fitting. No one here has to deal with their anxiety anonymously. Feeling alone in what they're going through is the reason most people come here in the first place. With that in mind, surely it makes sense to portray an image that is as far away from loneliness as is possible?'

I hear another murmur behind me, but this time it is accompanied by note-making and chair-swapping as people move around to chat with others while pointing at the video link.

'*Together* is how we do things here. *Together* is the way we get through the minefield that is anxiety, and together is how we can help change the perception of mental health forever...' Picking up the webcam, Alec turns around the screen to show the gathering of people in the room behind him. 'I, along with the many people in this room and thousands more online, have signed a petition. I believe there is a copy of that petition in front of each of you right now.'

The sound of papers rustling in the boardroom causes me to smile proudly. Not only do they have copies of the petition, they also have complete information packs containing written statements from Ruby, Aldo, Aidan and other members of the support group.

'Thousands of people have signed a petition that has only been open for a few short days. Given time, this could escalate to hundreds of thousands, if not millions. Now, those signatures are probably just names on a page to you, so here are a few of those who signed to speak for themselves...'

'Hello!' Yvette says cheerily, waving at the camera as though she is talking to a family friend. 'I'm Yvette Robinson and I attend Anxiety Anonymous. My daughter, Ruby, has been coming here for years and without your help, she wouldn't be where she is today and neither would I. This support group has given her the strength and courage to follow her dreams and believe in herself. For that, I thank you. However, the biggest thank you has to be for what you have done for me. Before I came here, I was ashamedly cold towards my daughter's suffering, but the support group introduced me to a whole community who could explain to me exactly what Ruby is going through.' Blinking back tears, Yvette smiles into the camera. 'I vote for Anxiety Together and so does Ruby.'

The webcam pans to other members of the group, who happily lap up the attention.

'Being part of Anxiety Anonymous has changed my life. It helped me to realise that I was not alone in what I was experiencing, at a time where I believed no one could ever help me. I vote for Anxiety Together.'

'This support group has taught me that I don't have to fight anxiety alone. I vote for Anxiety Together.'

'I vote for Anxiety Together.'

'I vote for Anxiety Together.'

'I vote for Anxiety Together...'

As person after person show their passion for the name change, I feel a lump form in the back of my throat. That is my support group up there. That is the amazing, brave, inspirational bunch of people I have grown to know and love. At first, most of those faces wouldn't dare to breathe a word and now look at them. They are shouting loud and shouting proud about their love for the support group.

Regardless of the outcome of this meeting, my mission is complete. People are standing tall and telling the world that the attitude towards mental health needs to change and that is exactly what I set out to do. All it takes it to plant the seed. It's like building a snowman. At first, the snowball is small, but the more you roll it, the bigger it becomes. The more people speak, the more people listen. Before you know it, you have built a platform that is impossible to ignore. The power to change lies in numbers and it would appear our numbers are growing by the second.

After waiting for Alec to give his closing words, I switch off the projector and turn to face the room for a final time.

'Anxiety drains sufferers of their happiness and takes away from their future, but *together* we can stamp it out. It's one word. One word with a whole world of meaning. Together. In union with other people. In union in the fight against anxiety. *Anxiety Together.*'

Finishing my speech with a subtle nod of the head, I wait for the round of applause to erupt and frown when a deafening silence comes back at me.

'Thank you, Sadie.' Clipboard guy says blankly. 'We'll be in touch...'

'And that's it?' Aidan says in disbelief. 'They really didn't say anything else?'

Swinging my legs over the edge of the cliff, I shake my head in response.

'Did they at least say when they would be in touch?' He persists, drawing a line in the ground with a tiny stone as the sun starts to lower in the distance.

'No, but the outcome doesn't really matter. I've started the ball rolling, that's the important thing. Every journey starts with a single step. If this was merely the first stop on the road to changing the way we tackle mental health, so be it.'

The rolling hills down below stretch out as far as the eye can see, making me feel on top of the world as I soak up every single detail. The woodland, the cottages, the stables that are providing horses with shelter for the night. It's captivating, even though I've seen it all a million times before.

'Sometimes, the smallest step in the right direction can lead to the biggest step of all. One small step is all it takes.' Aidan replies with a smile. 'One tiny step for Sadie, one giant leap for anxiety.'

I grin back at him, thinking of how that statement applies to most of life's situations. With just one tiny leap of faith, one little jump of courage, you can change your entire life. It might not seem that way on a day-to-day basis, but when you take a step back, you realise that *everything* has changed. You simply need to take a chance and never look back.

Enjoying the sensation of wind in my hair, I allow my eyes to close as the sun dips closer to the horizon, casting a cooling shadow over the two of us. Stealing a glance at Aidan, I notice he is doing the same. With his eyes closed and head tipped back, I can see every fine line on his face. Every laughter line and every frown line. Like a map of his life. The good times, the bad, the ups and the downs. It's all there, if you get close enough to see it.

He peels open an eye and I immediately look away, embarrassed that he caught me staring at him. Feeling his eyes burning into me, I bite my lip and toss a small twig into the air. Watching it fall into the abyss, I enjoy the sense of serenity that is settling in my stomach. The unknown is something that has always made me a little uncomfortable, but right now, I am completely okay with it. Instead of worrying about what is coming next, I am simply happy to go along with it and enjoy the ride.

The sky darkens a little more, reminding me that you need to have darkness in your life if you want to see the stars. You can't have a rainbow without a little rain and you can't have good without bad. The trick is being able to recognise something good when it's sitting right next to you...

Looking at Aidan out of the corner of my eye, I pretend not to notice his hand inching closer to my own. My pulse is perfectly steady as I calmly place my little finger on top of his. Feeling him instantly wrap his fingers around mine, I break into a smile when he turns to look at me. Without saying a word, Aidan returns to looking at the view with the same knowing smile on his face. Sometimes in life, silence can say more than words ever could. Just a meaningful look, a touch of the hand, or a knowing smile can tell you everything you need to know.

Two birds soar above us, dancing around one another beautifully as they chase the last of the sun. Their wings fade into the night, until all that is left is the memory of where they once were as the sky finally descends into complete darkness. One by one, hundreds of lights illuminate the villages below, creating a warm glow while we lie back and look up at the stars. The velvet blanket of black overhead is now displaying numerous twinkling stars. Each one teasing of a whole new world that is just waiting to be explored.

One star is outshining all the rest, making the others pale in comparison as it glints boldly, refusing to be ignored until its beauty is appreciated. Shuffling closer to Aidan, I rest my head on his chest and allow my eyes to relax on the stunning star. Its bright haze seems to ignite the entire sky as Aidan wraps his arm around my shoulders and suddenly I know. I know everything I have been waiting so long to be sure of.

It's time to start something new and trust in the magic of new beginnings...

Epilogue

Letting out a tired yawn, I stretch my arms over my head before making my way down the stairs. A squeaky step creaks beneath my feet as I rub my eyes sleepily and pause at the bottom of the staircase. A bunch of mail is splattered across the mat like confetti, just itching to be torn open. Bending down to retrieve them, I take a seat on the bottom step as Mateo rolls around next to my feet playfully.

Flipping through the cluster of letters, I clutch an official-looking envelope to my chest and allow the rest to fall to the floor. This is it. This is what I have been waiting for. Not daring to open it, I stare at the printed address with a racing heart before slowly slipping a finger beneath the seal. The crisp paper crinkles loudly as I straighten the letter in my hands and read the clear font carefully. The words appear to blur into one in my haste to process all the information at once.

> '...We are contacting in response to our recent meeting dated...
> ...We would like to take this opportunity to thank you for bringing this matter to our attention...
> ...Whilst we admire your dedication to raising awareness of mental health...
> ...Anxiety Anonymous has a long history dating back to...

...Anxiety Anonymous continues to reinforce our mission statement at every opportunity...
...Anxiety Anonymous continues to research new ways in which we can aid and influence...
...After much consideration, we have decided to **accept** *the proposed name change to Anxiety Together...'*

The letter continues to outline a suggested timeline and the relevant framework that will need to be addressed for the change to take place, but all I can focus on is that one line.

...After much consideration, we have decided to **accept** *the proposed name change to Anxiety Together...*

I've done it! I've really done it! My skin tingles with excitement as I clutch the paper tightly. With the help of the support group, I have changed the name of the charity forever. Not wanting to blink in case the letter disappears, I race back up the stairs in search of my phone to call Aldo. Snatching the handset from my duvet, I frantically jab at the keyboard as I retrace my steps. With the phone to my ear, I swing around the bannister and land on the mat next to the pile of letters.

As the line rings out, I zone in on a brown envelope with the word private stamped in block lettering across the front. Using my shoulder to hold the phone against my cheek, I pick up the letter and read the return address. *If undelivered, please return to O.L.E*

DNA Testing, London, SW2 1CC. Slowly ending the call, I retreat to the bottom step and tap the envelope against my hand.

Carefully tearing a hole in the corner, I peek inside before closing my eyes. They say when you don't know how you feel about a situation you should flip a coin, and while it is in the air you will know exactly what you're hoping for. Leaning over to the coat stand, I reach into my pocket and pull out a one pence piece. Everything in life is a gamble, but waiting won't change the dice. You either roll it or miss your turn.

The shiny coin glistens as I study both sides before tossing it into the air. Holding my breath, I smile when it lands effortlessly in the palm of my hand. The Queen winks back at me as I tear open the envelope, reminding me that what's meant to be will always find its way. In for a penny, in for a pound...

To be continued...

If you are struggling with anxiety, help is available to you.

Mind Infoline

0300 123 3393

Anxiety UK Infoline

08444 775 774

Anxiety United

www.anxietyunited.com

Follow Lacey London on Twitter

@thelaceylondon

Have you read the first two books in the Anxiety Girl series?

Anxiety Girl

Sadie Valentine is just like you and I, or so she was…

Set in the glitzy and glamorous Cheshire village of Alderley Edge, Anxiety Girl is a story surrounding the struggles of a beautiful young lady who thought she had it all.

Once a normal-ish woman, mental illness wasn't something that Sadie really thought about, but when the three evils, anxiety, panic and depression creep into her life, Sadie wonders if she will ever see the light again.

With her best friend, Aldo, by her side, can Sadie crawl out of the impossibly dark hole and take back control of her life?

Once you have hit rock bottom, there's only one way to go...

Lacey London has spoken publicly about her own struggles with anxiety and hopes that Sadie will help other sufferers realise that there is light at the end of the tunnel.

The characters in this novel might be fictitious, but the feelings and emotions experienced are very real.

Anxiety Girl Falls Again

So, what did Sadie Valentine do next?

After an emotional voyage through the minefield of anxiety and depression, Sadie decides to use her experience with mental health to help others.

Becoming a counsellor for the support group that once helped her takes Sadie's life in a completely new direction and she soon finds herself absorbed in her new role.

Knowing that she's aiding other sufferers through their darkest days gives her the ultimate job satisfaction, but when a mysterious and troubled man attends Anxiety Anonymous, Sadie wonders if she is out of her depth.

Dealing with Aidan Wilder proves trickier than Sadie expected and it's not long before those closest to her start to express their concerns.

What led a dishevelled Aidan to the support group?

As Sadie delves further into his life, her own demons make themselves known.

Will unearthing Aidan's story cause Sadie to fall back into the dark world she fought so hard to escape?

Join Sadie as she guides other sufferers back to mental wellness and battles her own torment along the way…

Meet Clara Andrews
Book 1

Meet Clara Andrews... Your new best friend!

With a love of cocktails and wine, a fantastic job in the fashion industry and the world's greatest best friends, Clara Andrews thought she had it all.

That is until a chance meeting introduces her to Oliver, a devastatingly handsome American designer. Trying to keep the focus on her work, Clara finds her heart stolen by Michelin starred restaurants and luxury hotels.

As things get flirty, Clara reminds herself that inter-office relationships are against the rules, so when a sudden recollection of a work's night out leads her to a cheeky, charming and downright gorgeous barman, she decides to see where it goes.

Clara soon finds out that dating two men isn't as easy as it seems...

Will she be able to play the field without getting played herself?

Join Clara as she finds herself landing in and out of

trouble, re-affirming friendships, discovering truths and uncovering secrets.

Clara Meets the Parents
Book 2

Almost a year has passed since Clara found love in the arms of delectable American Oliver Morgan and things are starting to heat up.

The nights of tequila shots and bodycon dresses are now a distant memory, but a content Clara couldn't be happier about it.

It's not just Clara things have changed for. Marc is settling in to his new role as Baby Daddy and Lianna is lost in the arms of the hunky Dan once again.

When Oliver declares it time to meet the Texan in-laws, Clara is ecstatic and even more so when she discovers that the introduction will take place on the sandy beaches of Mexico!

Will Clara be able to win over Oliver's audacious mother?

What secrets will unfold when she finds an ally in the beautiful and captivating Erica?

Clara is going to need a little more than sun, sand
and margaritas to get through this one...

Meet Clara Morgan
Book 3

When Clara, Lianna and Gina all find themselves engaged at the same time, it soon becomes clear that things are going to get a little crazy.

With Lianna and Gina busy planning their own impending nuptials, it's not long before Oliver enlists the help of Janie, his feisty Texan mother, to help Clara plan the wedding of her dreams.

However, it's not long before Clara realizes that Janie's vision of the perfect wedding day is more than a little different to her own.

Will Clara be able to cope with her shameless mother-in-law Janie?

What will happen when a groom gets cold feet?

And how will Clara handle a blast from the past who makes a reappearance in the most unexpected way possible?

Join Clara and the gang as three very different brides, plan three very different weddings.

With each one looking for the perfect fairy tale
ending, who will get their happily ever after...

Clara at Christmas
Book 4

With snowflakes falling and fairy lights twinkling brightly, it can only mean one thing - Christmas will be very soon upon us.

With just twenty-five days to go until the big day, Clara finds herself dealing with more than just the usual festive stresses.

Plans to host the perfect Christmas Day for her American in-laws are ambushed by her BFF's clichéd meltdown at turning thirty.

With a best friend on the verge of a mid-life crisis, putting Christmas dinner on the table isn't the only thing Clara has got to worry about this year.

Taking on the role of Best Friend/Therapist, Head Chef and Party Planner is much harder than Clara had anticipated.

With the clock ticking, can Clara pull things together - or will Christmas Day turn out to be the December disaster that she is so desperate to avoid?

Join Clara and the gang in this festive instalment and discover what life changing gifts are waiting for them under the tree this year...

Meet Baby Morgan
Book 5

It's fair to say that pregnancy hasn't been the joyous journey that Clara had anticipated. Extreme morning sickness, swollen ankles and crude cravings have plagued her for months and now that she has gone over her due date, she is desperate to get this baby out of her.

With a lovely new home in the leafy, affluent village of Spring Oak, Clara and Oliver are ready to start this new chapter in their lives. The cot has been bought, the nursery has been decorated and a name has been chosen. All that is missing, is the baby himself.

As Lianna is enjoying new found success with her interior design firm, Periwinkle, Clara turns to the women of the village for company. The once inseparable duo find themselves at different points in their lives and for the first time in their friendship, the cracks start to show.

Will motherhood turn out to be everything that Clara ever dreamed of?

Which naughty neighbour has a sizzling secret that she so desperately wants to keep hidden?

Laugh, smile and cry with Clara as she embarks on her journey to motherhood. A journey that has some unexpected bumps along the way. Bumps that she never expected...

Clara in the Caribbean
Book 6

Almost a year has passed since Clara returned to the big smoke and she couldn't be happier to be back in her city.

With the perfect husband, her best friends for neighbours and a beautiful baby boy, Clara feels like every aspect of her life has finally fallen into place.

It's not just Clara who things are going well for. The Strokers have made the move back from the land down under and Lianna is on cloud nine – literally.

Not only has she been jetting across the globe with her interior design firm, Periwinkle, she has also met the man of her dreams… again.

For the past twelve months Li has been having a long distance relationship with Vernon Clarke, a handsome man she met a year earlier on the beautiful island of Barbados.

After spending just seven short days together, Lianna decided that Vernon was the man for her and they have been Skype smooching ever since.

Due to Li's disastrous dating history, it's fair to say that Clara is more than a little dubious about Vernon being 'The One.' So, when her neighbours invite Clara to their villa in the Caribbean, she can't resist the chance of checking out the mysterious Vernon for herself.

Has Lianna finally found true love?

Will Vernon turn out to a knight in shining armour or just another fool in tin foil?

Grab a rum punch and join Clara and the gang as they fly off to paradise in this sizzling summer read!

Clara in America
Book 7

With Clara struggling to find the perfect present
for her baby boy's second birthday, she is
pleasantly surprised when her crazy mother-in-law,
Janie, sends them tickets to Orlando.

After a horrendous flight, a mix-up at the airport and
a let-down with the weather, Clara begins to
question her decision to fly out to America.

Despite the initial setbacks, the excitement of
Orlando gets a hold of them and the Morgans start
to enjoy the fabulous Sunshine State.

Too busy having fun in the Florida sun, Clara tries
to ignore the nagging feeling that something isn't
quite right.

Does Janie's impromptu act of kindness have a
hidden agenda?

Just as things start to look up, Janie drops a
bombshell that none of them saw coming.

Can Clara stop Janie from making a huge mistake,
or has Oliver's audacious mother finally gone too

far?

Join Clara as she gets swept up in a world of fast food, sunshine and roller coasters.

With Janie refusing to play by the rules, it looks like the Morgans are in for a bumpy ride...

Clara in the Middle
Book 8

It's been six months since Clara's crazy mother-in-law took up residence in the Morgan's spare bedroom and things are starting to get strained.

Between bringing booty calls back to the apartment and teaching Noah curse words, Janie's outrageous behaviour has become worse than ever.

When she agreed to this temporary arrangement, Clara knew it was only a matter of time before there were fireworks. But with Oliver seemingly oblivious to Janie's shocking actions, Clara feels like she has nowhere to turn.

Thankfully for Clara, she has a fluffy new puppy and a job at her friend's lavish florist to take her mind off the problems at home.

Throwing herself into her work, Clara finds herself feeling extremely grateful for her great circle of friends, but when one of them puts her in an incredibly awkward situation she starts to feel more alone than ever.

Will Janie's risky behaviour finally push a wedge

between Clara and Oliver?

How will Clara handle things when Eve asks her for the biggest favour you could ever ask?

With Clara feeling like she is stuck in the middle of so many sticky situations, will she be able to keep everybody happy?

Join Clara and the gang as they tackle more family dramas, laugh until they cry and test their friendships to the absolute limit.

Clara's Last Christmas
Book 9

The series has taken us on a journey through the minefields of dating, wedding day nerves, motherhood, Barbados, America and beyond, but it is now time to say goodbye.

Just a few months ago, life seemed pretty rosy indeed. With Lianna back in London for good, Clara had been enjoying every second with her best friend.

From blinged-up baby shopping with Eve to wedding planning with a delirious Dawn, Clara and her friends were happier than ever.

Unfortunately, their happiness is short lived, as just weeks before Christmas, Oliver and Marc discover that their jobs are in jeopardy.

With Clara helping Eve to prepare for not one, but two new arrivals, news that Suave is going into administration rocks her to the core.

It may be December, but the prospect of being jobless at Christmas means that not everyone is feeling festive. Do they give up on Suave and move on, or can the gang work as one to rescue the company that brought them all together?

Can Clara and her friends save Suave in time for Christmas?

Clara Bounces Back
Book 10

After taking control of Suave just six months ago,
Clara and the gang are walking on sunshine.
However, it's not long before the reality of owning
the business starts to hit.

With the repercussions of the Giulia Romano sex
tape still hitting the company hard, Owen starts to
question the stability of his investment.

Not wanting to give up on their dream, Clara and
her friends have one last shot at turning things
around before they throw in the towel for good.

When Marc spots a way to use the sex tape to their
advantage, Clara and the gang have no choice but
to put their future in the hands of her brazen
mother-in-law.

With a chickenpox epidemic taking over the group,
Janie's outrageous persona starts to cause friction
amongst Clara and her friends.

Can they trust Janie enough to act on behalf of the company, or will Janie's audacious behaviour be the final nail in the coffin for not only Suave, but their friendship with the Lakes?

Slip back into Clara's world and join the old gang as they reunite in this much-anticipated continuation of the Clara Andrews series!

Clara's Greek Adventure
Book 11

Janie, an eccentric billionaire and Mykonos.
What could possibly go wrong?

Almost a year has drifted by since Suave secured
the Ianthe contract and things are going very well
indeed.

With the success of the partnership shooting Suave
for the stars, the gang are closer than ever and
living life to the max.

Enjoying their new-found wealth proves to be a fun
and exciting time for Clara and her friends, but
there's one thing that's keeping a smile from
Oliver's face…

After declaring their love for one another twelve
months ago, Janie and Stelios have been loving life
in Stelios's luxury mansion in Mykonos, but not
everyone is happy for them.

Oliver has made no secret of his detest for Stelios

Christopoulos and that hatred seems to be growing stronger by the day. However, when the gang are invited to Mykonos to attend Stelios's exclusive Ice Party, Oliver has no choice but to put his own feelings aside and represent Suave.

Will this trip give Stelios a chance to finally win over Oliver?

Is Janie's love for Stelios based on more than just fast cars and money?

With five whole days under the Greek sun awaiting them, will they all leave as friends, or will the holiday be the final nail in the coffin for Oliver and his mother?

Join Clara and her friends as they jet to Mykonos, help a friend on the verge of a mid-life crisis and discover what Janie's heart really holds.

61295551R00175